TIDES OF PARADISE

MAUI ISLAND SERIES - BOOK 3

KELLIE COATES GILBERT

PRAISE FOR KELLIE'S BOOKS

"If you're looking for a new author to read, you can't go wrong with Kellie Coates Gilbert."
~**Lisa Wingate**, NY Times bestselling author of *Before We Were Yours*

"Well-drawn, sympathetic characters and graceful language"
~**Library Journal**

"Deft, crisp storytelling"
~**RT Book Reviews**

"I devoured the book in one sitting."
~**Chick Lit Central**

"Gilbert's heartfelt fiction is always a pleasure to read."
~**Buzzing About Books**

"Kellie Coates Gilbert delivers emotionally gripping plots and authentic characters."
~**Life Is Story**

"I laughed, I cried, I wanted to throw my book against the wall, but I couldn't quit reading."
~**Amazon reader**

"I have read other books I had a hard time putting down, but this story totally captivated me."
~**Goodreads reader**

"I became somewhat depressed when the story actually ended. I wanted more."
~**Barnes and Noble reader**

Copyright © 2022 by Kellie Coates Gilbert

All rights reserved.

No part of this book may be reproduced in any form or by any electronic or mechanical means, including information storage and retrieval systems, without written permission from the author, except for the use of brief quotations in a book review.

Tides of Paradise is a work of fiction. Names, characters, places, and incidents are either the product of the author's imagination or are used fictitiously, and any resemblance to actual persons, living or dead, is coincidental.

Cover design: Elizabeth Mackay

This book is dedicated to Emmie Sweetpea, my two and a half pound Yorkie, who has been on my lap daily since my first book was published.

ALSO BY KELLIE COATES GILBERT

THE MAUI ISLAND SERIES
Under The Maui Sky

Silver Island Moon

Tides of Paradise

The Last Aloha

THE PACIFIC BAY SERIES
Chances Are

Remember Us

Chasing Wind

Between Rains

THE SUN VALLEY SERIES
Sisters

Heartbeats

Changes

Promises

LOVE ON VACATION SERIES
Otherwise Engaged

All Fore Love

TEXAS GOLD SERIES
A Woman of Fortune

Where Rivers Part

A Reason to Stay

What Matters Most

STAND ALONE NOVELS

Mother of Pearl

Available at all retailers

www.kelliecoatesgilbert.com

TIDES OF PARADISE
MAUI ISLAND SERIES, BOOK 3

Kellie Coates Gilbert

1

"How could something so small create something so disgusting?" Shane held his tiny son's legs up in the air and positioned a diaper below the baby's bottom. Then he retched. Twice.

He looked over at his mom. "Uh...I think I need some help here."

Before Ava could respond, Aimee rolled her eyes at him and leaped from the chair where she sat. "For goodness sakes, Shane. You'd better not throw up on our kid." She moved to his side on the sofa and took over. When she'd finished fastening the diaper, she snapped the light-blue onesie back in place, then lifted the infant to her shoulder and patted his back lightly. Suddenly, the baby burped, leaving a glob on her shoulder.

"Oh, gross," Shane said, turning away. "Everything that comes out smells." He wretched again.

Aimee laughed and turned to face Shane's mother and sister. "Spit-up is my new fashion accessory."

Ava smiled. "Ah, I remember.

From across the room, Katie bounced little Noelle on her

knee. "Me, too. Now it's peanut butter in my hair." She laughed. "Welcome to parenthood, where going to the grocery store by yourself is now considered a vacation. And don't even get me started on labor. I was just glad I didn't poop on the table."

Shane's face twisted into a tight grimace. "Oh, please. Stop now. This conversation is taking a turn I don't want to be a part of."

The women in the room laughed.

"Oh, get over yourself," Aimee admonished with a wide smile. "You didn't go through nine hours of hard labor. The least you can do is listen with a little empathy."

"Men are such lightweights," Katie remarked. She leaned down to her toddler. "Take note, Noelle. Men are wimps and simply have no idea when it comes to all the things women have to deal with."

Noelle's dimpled hand lifted her shirt. "See my belly goat button?"

Katie rolled her eyes and pulled the pink shirt back over her daughter's bare tummy. "Honey, mannered women don't show their treasures in mixed company."

Noelle's eyes twinkled. "Me do."

Ava laughed loudly. "I think this one is going to grow up with a mind of her own."

"Like someone else we know?" Shane pulled a beer from the refrigerator and gave his sister a pointed look. "Katie, you want something?"

Katie glared back. "If you think that's an insult, Shane, I'll take it. I'm not ashamed to advocate for my beliefs and ideas. Knowing what you want and going after it isn't a character flaw." As if to punctuate her statement, she stuck her tongue out at her younger brother. "And, yes. I'll take that beer."

"So, how is the house coming along?" Ava asked, grinning.

Katie set her tiny daughter down on the floor to play. "With a little urging, the builders fast-tracked our project. We're only a few months from completion," she reported, ignoring the smirk on her mother's face. "And, yes. Jon and I have butted heads a couple of times," she admitted. "For example, he wanted granite countertops that had these swirls of blue...well, the name was actually steel gray. Believe me, they were blue. The marbled pattern was atrocious and didn't begin to match the look we are going for."

"We?" Shane asked as he handed his sister a beer.

Katie thanked him. "We...as in Jasmit Tan, our brilliant architect." Her face brightened. "He has an incredible eye for design. Simple lines. Colors from nature. He detests rudimentary and dysteleological elements."

Shane arched his eyebrows. "Wow...that's some big word there."

Katie ignored him. "Jasmit often has up to a nine-month waiting list. We were very fortunate to cement this relationship when we did."

"Yeah, I bet Jon feels really lucky," Shane muttered.

Ave turned to Aimee. "What about you? What are your long-term plans for housing? Rooming with Shane in that tiny shanty has got to feel crowded."

"It's all I can afford," Shane reminded. "Especially now that I have Carson. Do you even know what baby formula costs?" He shook his head. "And health insurance? I had to sell my bike in order to pay for that."

Aimee laid the now sleeping baby on her lap. She gently rocked her knees back and forth. "All that is true, Shane. Still, your living space is pretty tight." She turned to Ava. "The plan is for me to go back to work soon. The extra income will provide some options."

"We're hoping Aimee might be able to get her former waitressing job back." Shane ran a hand through the top of his hair "Of course, that'll mean added daycare expense."

"Raising a kid is not cheap, that's for sure...which is one of the main reasons we're cohabiting," Aimee added.

Ava sighed inside. She hated that Shane and Aimee were living together without being married. Sure, perhaps it was unfashionable to think like that in this day and age. She didn't care. Shane and Aimee had a little son. They should make a commitment.

Alani, her best friend and the local pastor's wife, thought the same and said so right to her son's face. "You can't expect God to bless anything you're not willing to do his way. His way is for a couple to covenant to *love, honor, and cherish each other...'til death do you part.*"

Ava knew from experience that vows could be broken. Still, she fully agreed with Alani and had floated her own subtle hints. "If money is an issue, I'll pay for the ceremony and reception. I could also help out with rent for a couple of months." She'd gladly lift her son's financial burden much longer, but Christel would have a fit. Her oldest daughter was a stickler for guarding Pali Maui's financial picture, which seemed to extend to Ava's personal bank accounts. Not to mention Christel, Katie, and even Aiden, had all followed their late father's belief that she often coddled Shane and had failed to let him grow up.

Coddled was too strong of a word. She was his mother and only wanted to assist in whatever way necessary when he needed help. Wouldn't any mother do that?

Regardless, Shane made it clear, in no uncertain terms, that it was far too early for Aimee and him to discuss the *forever* thing. Aimee had only been back on the island a short time. Even so, Ava hoped things would eventually head that way. Her mother's intuition told her that her son was head-over-heels infatuated with this girl. Despite his effort to hide the fact, Shane had moped for weeks after his girlfriend left to pursue an acting career in Los Angeles. Ava sensed her son was finally moving on, then Aimee showed up with her surprise bundle wrapped in a blue blanket.

Don't misunderstand. Their entire family was thrilled, of course. Well, maybe not thrilled. No one wanted Shane to be blindsided. These things should happen in the proper sequence—dating, engagement, marriage...then baby.

Yet life rarely went according to plan. The best you could do was to do the best you could do, with whatever came at you. She'd learned that after Lincoln had died. They all had.

Ava lifted from the sofa and headed for the kitchen. "Anyone hungry? I have some shrimp and cocktail sauce in the refrigerator."

When they all declined her offer, she got herself a banana out of the fruit basket and returned to the sofa and to her thoughts.

Plan or no...Ava couldn't help but wonder about the future. There was a lot to consider. Especially when it came to her children.

Ava supposed Christel would eventually marry Evan. Her daughter's relationship with the doctor seemed to be getting more serious by the day. Christel deserved that happiness, especially after her first marriage crumbled through no fault of her own.

Then there were Jon and Katie. Despite minor disagreements, their new place would be built soon. Fire had destroyed their former house, forcing them to live here at Pali Maui in one of the buildings designated for workers...affectionately known as the shanties. No doubt, their family would be glad to have a new, more spacious, place to call home.

Her oldest son, Aiden, was now settled in his new position as director of Maui Emergency Management Administration. The risk he'd taken saving the people on that boat, and the subsequent injuries he'd suffered, had cemented the notion he was the right candidate for the job. She couldn't be any prouder of what Aiden had accomplished at such a young age. It was only sad that his dad wasn't here to see it.

As for her, she was learning to be happy. Lincoln's death and the aftermath had taken a hit on her soul. It had taken time to find her footing. If she were completely truthful, his betrayal still stung. Despite all that, she intentionally grasped joy at every opportunity. Her heart was full.

And now, Shane was learning to be a daddy. She had a new grandchild to love on.

How could the Briscoes' future get any brighter?

2

Christel put the final touches on the quarterly report she had to provide to the bank in order to maintain their line of credit. Pali Maui was fortunate not to carry a long-term debt load. All the stakeholders in the pineapple plantation were family members and cash flow had been sufficient to fund most capital improvements. Even so, as chief financial officer, she thought it wise to establish a line of credit for emergency use.

Christel closed out the file and was in the process of shutting down her computer when her phone rang. She lifted her iPhone from her desk and pulled it to her ear. "Hey, Ori. This is a surprise. What's up?" Christel pinched the bridge of her nose. Staring at a computer screen for ten straight hours had taken a toll on her eyes.

"Morning, Christel. I hate to ask, but I need a favor."

"What's that?" She lifted from her office chair and stretched. The extended time sitting did her no favors, either.

Ori cleared his throat, clearly uncomfortable with what he was about to ask. "I wouldn't normally impose, but I'm in a bit of a crisis over here. I just got notified that one of the resort hotels over-ordered and they are willing to donate the food items to the center, but only if they can deliver this morning. I need able bodies to help unload. Everyone on my list has had to decline, including your siblings. Aiden is leading a training today. Shane is out on an excursion with your Uncle Jack. Katie has a meeting...something to do with her new house." He paused. "I'm desperate."

As tired as she was, Christel didn't give the matter any hesitation. "Of course, Ori. I'll come right away. I'll also see if I can round up some help."

Ori let out a sigh of relief. "Thanks, Christel. I can always count on you. I appreciate this."

Christel assured him it was no imposition. While that wasn't the entire truth—she still had a list of projects to get done—it was in her heart to help out, even if it wasn't convenient. Especially when it came to helping Ori.

She'd known the Kané family over her entire lifetime. Ori's twin sister had been her best friend and soul mate while growing up. They'd shared sleepovers, tubes of mascara, Backstreet Boys posters, and countless hours on the phone sharing their deepest thoughts.

Christel would never get over Mia's unforgiveable transgression, but she would do anything for her brother, who was known for giving the shirt off his back for anyone in need. Ori served as the director of Ka Hale A Ke Ola Resource Center, an establishment that provided emergency and transitional shelter and food for the homeless. The services also included counseling, medical care and child care for those in need.

"I'll see you in a little over an hour," Christel promised. She hung up and glanced at the wall clock, then grabbed her sunglasses from the top of her desk and headed for the door.

That's when an idea hit.

She jogged over to the shanty where Katie, Jon and their

family were staying temporarily until their new house was completed. A bit breathless, she rapped on the door.

Her niece answered.

"Hey, Aunt Christel. What are you doing here?" Willa stood holding a cereal bowl in her hand with a spoon perched inside. "Mom's not here."

"I didn't come over to see your mom. I came to see you," Christel explained. "Ori just called. He needs help unloading food donations and I thought I'd enlist you to come with me and help."

"Now?"

Christel grinned. "Yes, now. Go put the bowl in the sink and grab whatever you need. I'll make a Starbucks run on the way." Before her niece could object, she added, "And I'll text your mom and let her know you're with me."

While waiting for Willa, another idea formed. She pulled her phone and dialed Evan's office. The receptionist answered on the first ring. "Matisse Orthopedics. How can I help you?"

"Hey, Evelyn. It's Christel Briscoe. Is Evan out of surgery yet?"

"Yes, but I'm afraid he's not in the office. Said he had an errand. He's scheduled to return by late-afternoon, then he'll likely head to the hospital for rounds."

Christel swallowed her disappointment. "Oh, okay. Well, I guess I'll try to connect with him later tonight. Thanks."

"You're welcome, dear."

Christel closed out the call and pushed the phone in the back pocket of her jeans just as Willa bounded out of the back bedroom with a backpack slung over her shoulder. "Ready," she said. She noted Christel looking at the pack. "What? I'm bringing a few snacks. And my iPad."

Christel nodded slowly knowing her young niece rarely went without food and social media for any length of time.

On the way to the resource center, Christel looked across

the car seat at Willa, who had her head buried in her iPad. "Whatcha watching, Chick-a-Dee?"

Willa grinned. "TikTok videos. And are you ever going to quit calling me that?"

Christel hid her own smile. "Probably not."

"Like, are you going to be at my wedding someday and say, 'Ah...there goes Chick-a-Dee walking the aisle in her gown. Isn't she stunning?'"

"I might."

"Maybe I could name my first child that. Little Chick-a-Dee. Or, how about Chick-a-Dee Jr.? Or, maybe Chick-a-Dee, the second." Her niece laughed. "How does that sound?"

Refusing to be swayed, Christel simply nodded. "I like it."

She pulled into the Starbuck's drive-through. "What's your fancy? On me."

Without looking at the menu board, Willa quickly recited, "A Mocha Cookie Crumble Frappuccino with extra whip, extra drizzle, extra chips. And a cheese danish and a Birthday Cake pop."

Christel's eyebrows lifted. "Is that all?"

Again, without looking. "Yup."

Christel sighed. Oh, to be young again and not have to worry about calories. A crackly voice from the speaker box asked, "May I have your order?"

Christel leaned out the window. She recited her niece's order, then added, "And a Pike Place Roast."

"Size?"

"*Venti*, please." Yes, it was one of those mornings. She needed the extra caffeine. Especially after getting up at the crack of dawn to finish those reports.

Willa looked across the seat. "You don't have to do that, you know."

"Do what?"

"You don't have to lean out the window. Mom does that. You don't have to. They can hear you."

Christel eased forward in the line of cars. "Noted."

Familiar song lyrics blasted from Willa's iPad, drawing Christel's attention...something about Applebee's on a date night.

Christel leaned and watched the small screen as a group of girls with tops that barely covered their stomachs lunged their hips back and forth while they made a circular motion with their hands, all of them in unison. "Hmm...you know those girls?"

Willa glanced up. "Yeah, they're from my school. It's Amanda Cooper's channel."

Christel ran her fingers through the side of her short blonde hair, then checked her reflection in the visor mirror. "Her name sounds familiar. Wait!" She closed the visor. "Isn't that the girl who—?"

"Yeah," Willa said, cutting her off.

Christel frowned wondering if Katie knew her daughter was still hanging with this girl. Not likely.

Months back, Jon and Katie mistakenly thought a positive pregnancy test left in their bathroom had belonged to their daughter, only to discover it was Willa's friend, Amanda, who was pregnant.

"So, how is she?" Christel asked, trying to sound nonchalant.

Willa glanced over. "How's who?"

Christel pointed to the iPad. "Your friend."

Willa clicked off the video and stuffed the iPad back in her backpack. "She's not my friend."

Willa didn't give any details, but Christel suspected there was a story there. "Oh? I'm sorry to hear that."

"Don't be. She's not the kind of girl you want to be friends with."

Christel took a deep breath, deciding to push a little. "Is she...I mean, when is Amanda due?"

Willa leaned back against the car seat. "She's not pregnant anymore."

"Oh no, did she lose the baby?"

Willa just stared and didn't answer. Christel swallowed. "Oh."

She definitely needed to bring this up with Katie in the event she was unaware. Willa was at an age where a lot of things were coming at her pretty fast...adult things. Jon and Katie had their work cut out for them helping their daughter maneuver these teen years, and all that came with the prospect of growing up.

The line moved forward and Christel pulled her car up to the tiny open window. "Will that be cash or charge?" the girl inside asked.

Christel handed over her credit card in exchange for their order. She turned and pressed the sugar-laden drink into her niece's waiting hand. "Here you go, Chick-a-Dee."

Minutes later, they arrived at the Ka Hale A Ke Ola Resource Center. Christel cut the engine and she and Willa climbed out and headed inside.

Ori immediately greeted them with a wave. "Hey, thanks for coming. The delivery of this food donation was so last minute, it was hard rounding up people willing to assist in unloading the goods."

"No problem," Christel assured. "I snagged Willa to help."

Her niece tossed her empty drink container in a nearby trash can and glanced around. "Are we it?"

Ori nodded. "I'm afraid so. At least for now." As he said it, a large box truck pulled into the front parking lot. "Looks like they're here."

Ori handed Christel a couple of pairs of gloves. She handed one set to Willa, then rolled up her sleeves and slipped on her own pair. "Okay, you ready for this?" she asked her niece.

The front door opened and a girl who looked to be near Willa's age entered. She wore a pair of jeans shorts and a sleeveless white blouse. "Hey, Kina. What's up?" Ori asked.

The girl smiled as she made her way to a nearby table and grabbed a pair of gloves. "I'm here to help."

"Great," he said. "We can use all the hands we can get." He turned to Christel and Willa. "This is a new friend. She just moved here from Kaua'i."

The young girl nodded. "Yeah, we eat here sometimes. Me and my mom."

The news sobered Christel, and from the look on Willa's face, she was surprised to learn a girl her age needed the services offered at Ka Hale A Ke Ola Resource Center.

"Well, hey...nice to meet you." Willa smiled and waved for Kina to follow her outside. "We're just about to start unloading."

The four of them worked diligently over the next hour, unloading boxes filled with bags of rice and noodles, bricks of cheddar and swiss cheese, eggs, and packages of bacon and sausage. There were cases of orange and grapefruit juice and frozen bags of hash brown potatoes. Bulk bottles of ketchup and mustard. Cartons of milk. Frozen meat.

"Wow! What a load. This is great," Christel said as she positioned a box on a metal shelf in the storeroom.

"We're lucky. The resorts are very generous. I often suspect the managers over-order on purpose." Ori removed a glove and wiped his brow with his forearm. "People on the island are *lokomaikai*. It's not often we fail to have food and resources to deliver to those in need. Mia worked to start the resort donation program—" He immediately paused. "I'm sorry. I didn't mean to—"

Christel tossed him a weak smile. "That's okay. She's your

sister. Of course, you are going to mention her. And that's perfectly fine." She couldn't help herself from adding, "How is Mia?" She swallowed, wondering if she really wanted to know.

Ori's expression filled with compassion. "She's doing fine... considering." That's all he offered and Christel didn't prod for more information.

Her friend lifted another box. "Mom tells me Shane is a father. Is that true?"

The question was a simple one, yet Christel struggled to find a reply. "Yeah, you heard correctly," she finally confirmed. "I'm not sure what to say about the situation. I mean, the baby—his name is Carson—well, he's adorable. But I can't picture Shane as a dad, you know? He's still a kid himself."

Ori nodded. "Kids grow up. Shane will now have to move into adulthood with the rest of us."

Christel forced a weak smile. "Time will tell."

They headed out to the truck for the last of the boxes when a familiar car pulled into the parking lot and Evan got out.

Christel stood there holding a box, surprised at how the sight of him made her melt. She wasn't some school girl watching the football jock walk down the hall. Tell that to her insides.

He greeted them with an enthusiastic wave as he walked over. When near, he took the box from her arms. "Here, let me."

"What are you doing here?" she asked. "I understood you were busy most of the day."

"I have a donation coming." Even as he said the words, a blue and white haul-it-yourself van arrived. "I hope you need some bed linens. Seems the lady in hospital procurement ordered the wrong size. She was going to send the shipment back, but...well, I thought you could put them to use here at the center."

Ori grinned. "At somebody's personal expense, I suspect."

Evan looked dumbfounded. "I don't know what you could be talking about."

"Or who," Christel suggested. She reached and kissed Evan's cheek. Another reason to love this man.

The thought startled her. She'd never used the word *love* when thinking about Evan.

It had taken Christel a long time to get her head together after her divorce from Jay. She hid her struggle the best she could, but his addiction had taken its toll, and making the decision to end their marriage had been devastating.

Meeting Evan was a gift in many ways. Not only had he given her friendship, but he'd been so supportive after she'd finally shared about her marriage. He'd trusted her with the pain of losing Tess and his unborn son and told her how he feeling responsible for their deaths nearly buckled him. That kind of a connection was rare.

Evan seemed to be everything she needed and wanted, no question. Unlike Jay, he was steady and grounded. She didn't get side-kicked with his choices and behavior. Even more, Evan was amazingly handsome. He was tall and his shoulders and forearms portrayed physical strength, the kind you see in magazine models. He looked amazing in scrubs, or a suit. She loved his jeans and T-shirts best. Yet it was his nature that she found most attractive. Like the way he handled patients and their families with such understanding and compassion. When Aiden had his accident, her family was frantic. As her brother's doctor, he somehow instilled confidence that all would turn out well.

And it had. Largely, because of him.

Then there was that mesmerizing smile that quickly traveled to his eyes. One look and he had her.

Yes, there was a lot to love when it came to Evan Matisse. But did she *love* him?

Christel swallowed. It seemed her mind was betraying her

and had already darted ahead. Was she ready to take that step and move their relationship that close to the finish line?

"Who's Willa's new friend?" Evan asked, nodding across the room toward the girls who were in a giggly huddle, looking at the iPad.

"That's Kina," Christel explained. "Willa just met her but it looks like they are already fast friends."

Ori removed his gloves and leaned against a marred wooden desk piled with papers. "Kina is a great kid. Her mom's name is Halia Aka. They moved to Maui a few months ago with Halia's father, Chigger."

Ori grinned. "I met Chigger at the Olivine Pools. He's a disillusioned Vietnam vet who called the tropical Napali coast of Kaua'i home for many years. He told me that just before dropping his camouflage shorts and diving in the water naked." Ori released a small chuckle and lowered his voice. "They had a bit of a hard time transitioning and stayed here for a few weeks. Unfortunately, Chigger decided to return to the commune on Kaua'i convinced that capitalism still stinks after his dream of making marijuana chocolates fizzled. Halia and Kina stayed on."

"Where do they live now?" Christel asked, curious.

"She's living with three other women in a loft above a boutique in Pa'ia. One of the women inherited a plot of land nearby, and together, the roommates have started a day retreat for women. They call it Banana Patch, in part because of the banana palms on the property, and in part after a commune by that name here on Maui that folded years ago."

Evan casually draped his arm around Christel's shoulder. "A day retreat?"

Ori nodded. "It's actually a wellness retreat that can last multiple days. Women pay to spend time relaxing in the beauty of a calm environment. They learn new skills focused on mental peace and enjoy healthy treatments like massage and salt baths." He laughed again. "I'm not sure they make a lot of profit. The ladies are prone to giving the services away to anyone who can't afford to pay, which is nearly all their patrons."

Christel found herself amused. "Halia sounds like a real earth mother."

Ori sighed. "The earthiest. But who am I to judge? Blessed are those who wear henna tattoos and burn incense—"

"For they shall inherit tranquility and harmony of soul," Christel said, laughing. "Who couldn't stand a little of that?"

3

Katie woke from a dead sleep to Jon's snoring. She stared at the ceiling in the dark for several moments before lifting from her pillow, frustrated. She looked over at her sleeping husband.

How could he not wake himself up? He sounded like a grizzly dancing with a hyena.

She poked him with her elbow...hard. "Jon. Turn over." She waited. "Jon," she repeated, this time a little louder. "Turn over."

Still nothing.

"Jon!" she nearly shouted. "Wake up and turn over."

"Huh? What?" Her husband lifted his head and looked around in confusion.

Katie turned on the bedside lamp. "You were snoring. Again."

Jon sat up and pinched the bridge of his nose. "Sorry. I guess I can't help it."

"Well, you're going to have to do something. I can't sleep. Maybe we should look into getting you one of those CPAP machines." Up until now, Katie had been reluctant to suggest such a thing. How sexy would that be? Then again, snoring wasn't exactly attractive, either.

Jon looked at her like she'd lost her mind. "Can I go back to sleep now?"

She rolled her eyes. "Only if you use two pillows." She tossed him the extra she used. "Tomorrow, I'll order you one of those pillows from the guy on television."

Jon positioned the second pillow under his head. "I thought you said you were never going to order online again," he mumbled.

True. Statistically, she returned far more items than she kept. A waste of time, in her opinion.

"I don't. But we can't go on like this. Lack of sleep affects my ability to work." She punched her pillow and flopped her head down. Then she remembered the light.

After turning off the lamp, Katie nestled in and tried to fall asleep. She tossed. And turned. Finally, she gave up and returned to staring at the ceiling. When Jon began to snore again, she'd had enough and went to the bathroom and flicked on the light.

On the way to the toilet, she padded past the tiny sink and glanced in the mirror. The image looking back at her was not pretty. There was a time when she would've been horrified to see her hair matted, her face mottled. She sure wouldn't have wanted Jon to see her like that and would have taken a few minutes to repair the nighttime damage with a dab of makeup and a comb.

That was back then.

Now, all that mattered was doing her business and returning to bed.

Before sliding back under the covers, she realized she'd forgotten to take her vitamins...a ritual she never skipped.

Sighing, she slid her feet into her slippers and quietly made her way across the dark room. About halfway to their bedroom door, Jon's snoring grew louder.

Katie kept her jars of vitamins in the kitchen, in a clear plastic container on the top shelf in her pantry out of the reach of little hands, right next to the containers of flour and sugar. Her shelves were orderly, with boxes of cereal, rice and cake mixes arranged by size. Her canned goods were alphabetical and the bottles of sauces lined up by ethnicity. The Southern barbeque sauces were first, followed by bottles of soy sauce, sesame oil and peanut sauce. Next came the tiny jars of salsa and extra bottles of hot pepper sauces. She liked Tabasco. Jon preferred Cholula.

She'd often been teased about her propensity for having a place for everything, and everything in its place. Once, her brothers pulled a prank and scrambled her system by mixing jars with boxes and placing bottles of ketchup next to her vitamins. She'd paid them back a few months later by offering them a plate of Oreo cookies where she'd gleefully replaced the white frosting center with white toothpaste.

No one messed with Katie Ackerman!

Regardless, she believed that an hour spent organizing could save her two hours of searching. That was especially so in this tiny house. It was simply a matter of efficiency.

She turned on the kitchen light and padded across the floor. After doling out her vitamins into the palm of her hand, she filled a glass at the sink. That's when she noticed something outside the window.

She quickly turned off the light and leaned to the window for a better glimpse. No, she wasn't snoopy. Only curious.

In the light from above the neighboring door, Katie could see her Aunt Vanessa laughing.

Was that a guy with her? Oh, my goodness, it was!

And he was a hottie. Even from this distance, Katie could see now tall he was, she'd guess about six-two, at least. He had broad shoulders, thick dark hair, a chiseled jawline like you'd see on a film star.

Way to go, Aunt Vanessa!

The man leaned and cupped her aunt's chin in his hands, bent and whispered something against her ear, then he kissed her...a kiss that went on for several minutes.

Katie watched, mesmerized.

It'd been a long time since she'd been kissed like *that*.

Her mind quickly recalled many nights standing at her parents' front door after a date with Jon. Memory of the way he looked at her before kissing her goodnight still brought tingles to her toes. Back then, they couldn't seem to keep their hands off each other.

She met Jon at a party, one of those events she rarely attended. Her friend, Heather, had begged her to go. Heather was over-the-moon infatuated with some guy she'd met on the beach the night before and wanted to accept his invitation to the party but was too afraid to attend alone.

"Please," she begged. "It's on the beach. Besides, I'll pay you back. Promise." Her eyes lit up. "Tell you what, I'll go to the bookstore with you tomorrow. We'll browse the romance aisle. You'd like that, right?"

For years, paperbacks with bare-chested man covers had been her hidden pleasure, a secret she'd only shared with Heather.

Katie shook her head, a bit reluctant. "I don't know. Those kinds of parties wear on me pretty fast. I hate loud music where you can't even hear yourself talk. I always leave with a headache."

In the end, she folded. It was either that or be woken up and have to sneak out of her parents' house to go get Heather when she'd had too much to drink and couldn't drive. After reading far too many tragic news stories, Katie had forced a pact between them months earlier promising they would never let the other take a chance on the road if they were even slightly inebriated. She now had a similar pact with Shane. One call and she'd drop everything and come.

She and Heather were at the party only a few minutes before Heather whisked off with that new guy. Feeling out of place, Katie bumped her way to a makeshift bar constructed of plywood placed on top of two rickety looking sawhorses. A couple of pimply-faced guys, who didn't look old enough to drive a car, let alone drink, stood dutifully dispensing beer from a silver keg.

Upon approach, one of them offered a red plastic cup with white froth overflowing the rim. "Hey, you're pretty. Are you here alone?"

He said something more, but Katie suddenly couldn't make out the words over top of the music that was now blasting only a few yards from her. "Do you have any water?" she shouted.

"What?"

"Water! Do you have any?"

The kid looked at her like she had two heads. Either he hadn't heard her or water wasn't on the menu. "Never mind," she said and turned to see if she could catch a glimpse of Heather somewhere in the building throng of kids.

She set out through the crowd, getting bumped and jostled. Another reason she detested these things.

Not finding Heather, she turned, thinking she might simply wait in the car. When she did, she nearly face-planted into a guy's chest. "Oh, excuse me," she apologized.

The full moon lit one side of his face, his jawline a shadow across his neck. His disheveled hair was the color of walnuts, and a thin layer of stubble covered his lower face. He was a strange combination of the boy next door and a pirate on the sand holding a wench by the waist.

Her breath caught as she felt her insides breaking loose.

He laughed. "You look like you need rescuing."

"Are you calling me helpless?" she challenged, but with a smile.

"Oh, no. You look to be fairly fierce. But clearly uncomfortable." He tilted his head and handed her his half-empty red cup. "And you appear thirsty."

She didn't want the beer. She grinned and took the cup anyway.

"Look, these crowds aren't really my thing. Want to go for a walk?" he asked, his eyes clearly hopeful she'd say yes.

"On the beach?" She took a sip of the beer and handed the cup back.

Laughing, he nodded toward the sky. "No, I thought we might stroll the moon." His jean shorts were ripped a little above the knee and he wore a wrinkled white button-down shirt...open at the chest.

She drew in a deep breath of the night-blooming jasmine that bordered the shoreline. Normally, she'd have a smart retort. A few words that would put him in his place. When she opened her mouth, nothing came out. Something about that chest made her drop her mental rocks. "I'd like that...beach or moon."

From day one, she felt heat whenever she was within a few feet of Jon. He felt the same. They found ways to be together every day and when they were physically apart, they were on the phone at every opportunity. She couldn't get enough of him.

Katie now braced against the kitchen sink to steady herself. A subterranean shift moved beneath her feet as she realized how much she missed feeling like that. Sure, they still enjoyed being together behind closed doors. But it was different now. They were married. Had two kids. A dog. Car payments.

And Jon snored.

When exactly had everything changed?

It was then that she realized she was still holding the vitamins in her hand. She tossed them in her mouth and took a drink, pushing them down. Then, she placed the glass in the dishwasher, turned, and headed for the bedroom with stone-hard determination. That boy on the beach was still hers. Her blood ran warmer the instant she knew all she had to do was turn the situation around. Last she knew, she still had the touch that sent her husband in a spin.

She eased the bedroom door open and slipped to the Jon's side of the bed, not even hiding the grin on her face as she contemplated her next move.

Suddenly, Jon's mouth fell open and he let out a long, drawn-out snore...one that could wake people on Oahu.

Katie groaned. All amorous thoughts puddled at her feet.

With a heavy sigh, she dropped her plan and shuffled around to her side of the bed and climbed inside. Curling under the covers, she once again stared at the ceiling. A dull-edged pain filled her.

Why was the beginning of the romance story always better than the following chapters?

4

A light rap at Ava's office door drew her attention. She looked up from the paperwork on her desk to see Alani's face peeking through the cracked door.

"Am I interrupting?" her friend asked.

"Not at all," Ava said, waving her in. "It's nearly lunchtime. I welcome the break."

Alani grinned. "I was hoping you'd treat me to one of Jon's menu items." She motioned at her outfit. "I needed an excuse to show off my new pants."

Ava stood and came around her desk. "Oh, Alani. I love the print. And the colors." Her plus-sized friend often wore bright-colored muumuus. Slipping into a pair of pants was likely a step out of her comfort zone. "I mean it. You look really nice."

"I do, don't I?" She twirled around, further showing off the flowing fabric. "And I bought two more pair in different prints."

That's what Ava loved about her best friend. Not only was she perpetually in a good mood, she wasn't afraid to embrace change. She'd even bounced back from her daughter's betrayal faster than Ava could ever have imagined. Mia's relationship with Lincoln had cut all of them deeply. Alani hurt, but never let those emotions sweep her out to sea.

"So, what do you say?" Alani asked. "Are you taking me to lunch? Your treat?"

Ava laughed. "How can I turn down such a fabulous offer?"

No Ka 'Oi was known for having a reservation list that booked up months in advance. Despite the popularity of the farm-to-market restaurant, management saved one table for unique situations, which often included serving family and friends.

Jon greeted them as soon as they walked through the open walkway and stepped to the maître d podium. "Well, how's my favorite mother-in-law?" He leaned and brushed Ava's cheek with a kiss. "Alani, you're looking as good as always." He gave her plump shoulders a tight hug, then led the two of them to a table out on the sprawling rock-floored lanai with a view of the ocean in the distance. "Best table for my best girls." He pulled a chair out and seated each of them.

Alani grinned and pointed her thumb across the table at Ava. "She's buying...so hit us with the most expensive dish you've got." Her laughter caused deep dimples to form at the sides of her mouth.

"For you two, only the finest. And everything is on the house," John assured. "Today, we're serving rosemary smoked ahi, lightly seared, with a side of mango and pineapple salsa over rice."

"Sounds delicious, Jon." Ava smiled and pointed to the vase at the center of the table. "Where in the world did you get two-toned curcumas? These are some of my favorites, but are so hard to find."

"Ask your daughter. As you know, Katie is very resourceful."

Ava nodded. "That she is." She turned to Alani. "At four, Katie was determined she wanted to drink coffee so she marched up to a Starbucks counter and ordered her own *crappocino*."

They all laughed.

After Jon left the table, Alani placed a linen napkin across her new pants. "So, how is Katie? How's the house build coming along?"

"The project is progressing just fine," Ava reported. "And Katie? Well, she's driving us all crazy with the details. My girl holds the title *Drama Queen of Pali Maui*. The tile for the showers didn't arrive as scheduled and she nearly had a meltdown. She went on and on about it yesterday and only calmed down when Vanessa shoved a cold soda in her hand and told her to take a chill pill." Ava laughed. "In my humble opinion, that exchange was the pot calling the kettle, if you get my drift."

"How is your sister? I'm a little surprised you haven't killed each other by now. Seriously, I get up every morning and check the news."

"Now who's being the drama queen?" Ava said with a chuckle. "And Vanessa is fine. More than fine. She's dating."

Alani reached for her water goblet. "Oh? Who's the lucky guy?"

"Guys. She's dating multiple men...sometimes two a day. I'm surprised my sister doesn't keep an appointment calendar to keep from overbooking."

Alani reached for her water glass. "Good for her! No one should be alone." She paused. "What about you, Ava? I know it's early yet. But do you think you will ever be open to having another man in your life?"

The question was innocent enough. Still, Ava shuddered at the thought. "Absolutely not. My life is full enough, thank you. I have my children, and grandchildren...which now includes a new baby. And then there's Pali Maui. While Lincoln didn't shoulder much of the day-to-day operation, the marketing he normally took care of is now on my plate as well."

"Can't Christel take some of that over?"

"Christel is in a new relationship and that is filling her time, so I don't want to impose on her to add more to her duties. She had such a rough time after Jay. I'm really happy to see her thriving, know what I mean? Besides, I'm not complaining. I love my family and my work. It's plenty enough to keep me content."

Alani looked at her with skepticism. "You say that now, Ava, but you're young. I hope you might feel differently in a few years. I love Elta very much. No one could ever replace that dear man. Even so, if the Lord took him home, I'd be open to another relationship. I'd wish the same for him...if something were to happen to me. Life is too short to be alone."

Ava waved her off. "Maybe so. Things are different for me." Especially after Lincoln's betrayal, she thought. How would she ever trust again? She wouldn't.

The server arrived at their table. She placed plates of arugula salad topped with roasted beets and pear slices on the table. "Your entrees will be out soon," she told them.

Ava was quick to dig in. She was starving. "Oh, before I forget...Vanessa met some gal at the farmer's market the other day. Apparently, they became friendly. An unlikely pair, if you ask me. Her name is Halia Aka. She runs a women's wellness center called the Banana Patch. Vanessa signed us up for a class next week. Why don't you join us?" Ava urged. "I hate those kinds of things."

"If you hate it, why are you going?" Alani dug her fork into a beet. "Even more, why are you asking me to share in the pain?"

"Two reasons. In answer to your first question, there are so few things I have in common with Vanessa. I thought it might be a way for us to connect."

Alani gave her head a slight nod. "Sounds reasonable...and commendable, given the history with your sister. What's the other reason?"

Ava paused and held her fork midair. "Halia's daughter is Willa's new friend. Willa says Halia and Kina are new to the island and they're having a tough go of things. Apparently, they live with several other women in some loft in Pai'a and barely earn enough to live on."

"Oh, I know who you're talking about. That's the same mother and daughter Ori mentioned to me and Elta. They showed up at Ka Hale A Ke Ola a few months ago. When Ori told us about their situation, the church helped them financially."

"Then I can count on you to go with me?" Ava gave her a look. "If not for your best friend, then for the bigger cause?"

"I don't know. Attending a class at a wellness center sounds as much fun as going to the dentist."

"Oh, come on. I hate the idea, too. All the more reason to attend together...for support."

Alani pushed a bite of salad into her mouth and chewed, thinking it over. Finally, she swallowed. "Okay, I'll go. But only because you're my best friend."

Two days later, Ava and Alani loaded up in the car with Vanessa and they headed for Pai'a. As they drove into the trendy coastal community, Alani grinned from the back seat. "Where is this place?"

Vanessa held up her phone. "I put the address Halia provided into this GPS app."

"What road?" Ava asked.

"Why?" Her sister held up her phone. "This will direct us there."

"If you simply give me the address, I'll find it."

Vanessa opened her mouth to argue, then paused, took a deep breath, and cited the address. "It's on Baldwin Road."

Alani leaned back in her seat. "You okay, Ava?"

"Yes. I am a bit preoccupied. I found out late last night that one of our shipments was late...again. I'm going to have to work to replace them. This has happened far too often. With Lincoln gone, I think they believe they can take advantage."

Alani chuckled. "They'll soon learn that notion is miscalculated. Between you and Christel, you'll have them recalibrated in no time."

"I'm not into second chances. If a business partner can't be trusted, they need replaced."

Vanessa raised her eyebrows. "Sounds like you need this retreat."

Ava tightened her grip on the steering wheel. She could think of several retorts, not all of them kind. She had to remind herself of her goal—the reason she'd decided to come to this silly thing in the first place. She wanted to mend her relationship with her sister.

Minutes later, they pulled onto a long gravel road that winded through thick stands of banana palms, sugar cane palms, and clusters of cana topped with bright red blooms. Suddenly, the view opened to a spacious area with a large wooden structure surrounded by pools of water. A foot bridge led to the entry.

Alani craned her neck for a better look. "Wow. This is nicer than I expected."

Ava thought so as well. She wasn't sure what she expected, but her mood immediately improved.

"Halia and her business partners have worked really hard to get the place in shape. Apparently, the entire site was pretty rundown. They were on a tight budget. It's amazing what paint and some landscaping can do," Vanessa said.

Ava opened the car door and climbed out. "This isn't just a little landscaping. Someone has real talent. It's beautiful."

Alani agreed. "I feel more peaceful already."

"That would be the result of Halia's hard work," Vanessa told them. "She told me it took her all summer to get the place in shape. She even installed the pools using a YouTube video for instruction."

Ava was duly impressed. "Well, if she ever needs an extra job, send her to Pali Maui. I'm sure Katie would love to work with her. She's always looking for ways to heighten the appeal for her tours."

The front door opened and out stepped a woman in perhaps her early forties. She was tall and lanky, wore a caftan embroidered at the neckline and down the arm openings. Her long dark hair was braided to the side, and simple silver geometric drops dangled from her ears. She wore no makeup and had a lovely smile. "Welcome to Banana Patch," she said, waving them all inside.

Vanessa gave her friend a hug. "This place is so much more than you described. Halia, it's really nice."

"Well, we still have a lot of work to do. But over time, we'll accomplish everything we need to." Her voice was soothing and melodic.

Ava looked around. True, the interior was not as worthy of applause. There were bare-beamed rafters and walls. Wooden floors were scattered with woven rugs. The furniture was simple and utilized fabrics that looked woven by hand. An indoor fountain was embellished with a live parrot on a stand. "Welcome. Welcome," the bird said loudly as it bobbed its head up and down.

Ava jumped back in surprise. "Oh my!" Her hand went to her chest. "I didn't expect that."

Their host grinned. "That's Coconut."

Vanessa came closer, her eyes bright. "That parrot would make a great television segment. Viewers love that kind of thing." Then, as if remembering she no longer had a job at a station, she sighed.

"We are so glad you've joined us. Vanessa has told me so

much about the two of you." Halia seemed barely able to curb her enthusiasm.

Ava glanced over at Alani, who returned a silent warning signaling she, too, was wondering what Vanessa has said about the two of them.

Halia turned to Alani and reached for her hand, covering it with her own. "It goes without saying how much I adore Ori. Without his help, and yours, well..." Her eyes grew misty. "May the universe pay you back abundantly."

"Banana Patch is curated to provide a one-of-a-kind experience designed to elevate your personal frequencies to restore you to the highest levels of health, wellness, and mindset." She gave a reassuring smile. "During your stay, you'll enjoy daily yoga and meditation designed to further this healing process. We urge you to embrace this opportunity to steep yourselves in nourishing light, taking time to be still, to move less, and to soften your inner spirit."

Another woman entered the room from behind a draped doorway followed by a strong scent of incense. She extended a woven basket. "I'm Tikira. Please place all electronic devices in the basket. They will be returned to you at the end of the retreat."

Ava immediately shook her head in protest. "I'm afraid I can't do that. I'm expecting some very important communications from a new shipper we are talking with and—"

Vanessa reached inside Ava's purse, pulled out her cell phone, and started tapped away on her screen.

Ava's hand struck out to grab her phone back from her sister. "What are you doing?"

"I'm texting Christel." *Bleep,* came the reply. Vanessa grinned and dropped the cell in the basket. "Chill, Ava. It's only two days."

"Two days? No one said this was an overnighter!" She glanced at Alani. She simply shrugged.

Her sister explained that robes and pajamas were provided. "This time away will do you good. Besides, Christel can take care of things back at Pali Maui. You mentioned just the other day how capable she was, how much you relied on her now that Lincoln is gone." Vanessa reached for her own phone and tossed it in the basket. "Two days, Ava. Surely you can unplug for that short length of time."

The parrot bopped its head. "Two days. Only two days."

Ava gave the parrot a dirty look, then focused the same on her sister. Alani glanced between the two of them, looking a bit worried.

"Okay," she consented. "But we're not staying two full days. We're leaving tomorrow morning right after breakfast."

"Or, maybe a little later," Vanessa pushed.

Halia patted Alani on the back. "Tikira will take you to your rooms. I'll give you some time to settle in and then I'd ask you to join the rest of the guests out by the labyrinth." She pointed out the open sliding doors to an intricately designed pathway made of ankle-high boxwood shrubs that had been shaved with precision. "We'll be doing a walking meditation to clear our conscience and aide in inner reflection."

As they followed Tikira, Ava leaned to Alani and whispered, "I'm guessing we'll be painting gourds before we're through."

Alani whispered back, "Do you think they'd get offended if I pull out my Bible and read scripture instead?"

The sleeping porch, as they called it, was a complete surprise—even to Vanessa. It had been a while since any of them had slept in a communal situation. Even in Ava's college dorm, there were only two of them. Somehow, she was now expected to sleep with eight women, including her. She wasn't happy about it and quickly let Vanessa know.

"Do you think I'm happy about sleeping on a slab of wood

with a thin mattress?" Vanessa countered, her voice low so as not to be overheard.

When Halia looked their way, the three of them simply smiled.

Alani quickly whispered, "Let's just make the best of it. It'll be like having a junior high sleepover."

"My bones are well past junior high age," Ava reminded, this time forgetting to lower her voice.

"Is everything okay?" Halia asked with her hands folded in front of her stomach. All things considered, Ava was sure Kina's mother was nice and all, but she was definitely out there. Ava wouldn't be a bit surprised if she ate wheatgrass for breakfast.

After getting settled, they joined the rest of the retreat guests for a yoga class. Despite what was promised in the brochure, Ava soon learned the yoga lifestyle wasn't all green smoothies and inner peace.

From the look on Alani's face as she attempted her first Downward Dog, she wholly agreed. "Do you think it would be rude if stop doing this nonsense," she asked. "Because I'm afraid I'm going to accidently fart." Alani turned her red-faced head and nodded in Vanessa's direction. "And who does your sister think she is? Yoga Queen?" She shook her head. "I mean, surely her undies are going to tourniquet her buttocks if she doesn't stop doing those Crescent Lunges."

Ava couldn't help herself. She spit with laughter. This merited a frown from the instructor.

When the session finally ended, a loud bong signaled it was time for lunch. Ava was starved. Unfortunately, a hot cheeseburger and fries, which was what she most craved, was not on the plate set before her. Instead, the meal consisted of some sort of taco with a side that appeared to be sauteed leeks sprinkled with sunflower seeds.

Ava frowned in the direction of Alani. "What is this?" She pointed to the taco.

"I don't care," her best friend answered. "I'm so hungry I could eat a horse." Alani pulled the taco from her plate and pulled it close to her mouth. She quickly let it drop back on the plate. "Oh, ugh. This smells like a horse. You don't think...?"

Vanessa rolled her eyes. "Don't be silly. The menu is entirely vegan."

Halia appeared carrying a large pitcher. "Do any of you care for some spring water?" she asked. "The water is infused with cucumber and mint."

Alani forced a smile. "Yes, thank you."

Ava took a breath and pointed to her plate. "Uh, I'm afraid I didn't have a chance to look over today's menu. Could you tell me what this is?"

Halia nodded with enthusiasm. "Of course! Those are lentil tacos with cashew sour crème and vegan cheese. The shells are actually Indian Tosai, a thin crepe-like pancake made with fermented rice."

Ava swallowed. She'd pass.

"The food here is entirely holistic and will cleanse your body of toxins," Halia explained.

Vanessa slowly pushed her plate aside. "Yeah, I get that ridding the toxins is important, but do you have anything else? I'm allergic to rice. And lentils. And maybe even cashews."

"Oh, I'm sorry. We don't," Halia apologized.

Vanessa gave her a weak smile. "I have a candy bar back in my room."

Halia filled Vanessa's glass. "Or, you could wait until dinner. Fasting is extremely good for you. We'll be having creamy carrot pasta sauce over noodles tonight. Our guests rave over that entrée."

Ava handed over her water tumbler. As Halia filled the glass, she smiled at their host. "Your retreat center is lovely."

That seemed to make Halia happy. She smiled and filled the remaining water glasses. "I hope you'll visit us again soon."

When she was out of earshot, Alani leaned over. "It's a sin to lie, you know."

Ava shrugged. "I hoping for a little grace."

Vanessa struck up a conversation with a young woman sitting on the other side of the table, a woman who was thin and beautiful and looked entirely at home eating lentil tacos.

Ava reached for her water glass and lowered her voice. "I bet there are no toxins in that petite body."

Alani laughed. "Hey, regardless of how this retreat is going, I just want you to know I'm proud of you."

"Proud of me? Why?"

"I know your relationship with Vanessa has not been entirely easy over the years. Despite your history, you've really stepped up and tried to mend the situation. It seems to be working."

"Why? Because we're not at each other's throats?" Ava asked, staring at the concoction on her plate.

"Yes, in part. But you've shown Vanessa how to put others before herself. From what you've told me, that's not always been her *modus operandi*."

Ava sighed. "Well, I appreciate the sentiment, but don't take out any billboards announcing the big makeover yet."

"What do you mean?"

"I mean, it's difficult for a striped tiger to grow spots."

A buzzing sound drew their attention. Vanessa excused herself from her conversation and drew her arm up. She pressed a button on her watch. "Hey, Scott. I was hoping you'd call. Last night was...well, it was perfect."

Ava scowled at sister. "What the heck? I thought there was a 'no-phone' policy."

"Hang on for a minute, will you, Scott?" Vanessa grinned and covered the tiny speaker with her other hand. "No phones, perhaps. But I didn't hear anyone say we couldn't wear an Apple watch."

Ava gave Alani a pointed look, arched her eyebrows, and whispered, "No worries. I hear stripes are in this season."

5

As much as Aiden adored his work at the Maui Emergency Management station, especially now that he'd been promoted to captain, he was still happy when the big clock on the wall signaled his shift was over.

The last eight hours had been challenging. A three-car collision on the road to Hana required use of the jaws of life tool to extricate two passengers. The incident immediately brought back painful memories of the accident which took the life of his father. For the most part, Aiden could successfully hide those gut-wrenching images from his conscience—until something like today forced him to relive the worst night of his life, a heavy mental souvenir he'd had to put down.

Thankfully, the incident today had turned out much better. Both passengers were transported to Maui Memorial with non-life-threatening injuries. Still, the emotional trauma left Aiden wiped out. All he wanted was to get home, grab a beer, and chill.

He'd just clocked out when he saw his brother walking toward him. "Hey, Shane. What are you doing here?"

"Yeah, bruh. I figured this would be a surprise."

Aiden positioned his baseball cap on his head and pointed to the door. "Well, timing is great. I just clocked out."

Outside, the sun was bright and the air carried a hint of cool breeze. Aiden and Shane headed in the direction of their vehicles in silence. Finally, Aiden couldn't stand the suspense and turned to his brother. "So, you want to tell me what's up?"

Shane let a little grin escape his lips. "I need your help."

"Yeah. With what?"

Shane stopped in front of his car and ran his hand over the top of his head. "Can you keep this to yourself?"

"Yeah, sure."

Shane shuffled on his feet a bit before spitting out what he wanted. "Dude, I need you to go shopping with me."

Aiden's eyes widened. "Shopping?"

"Jewelry shopping."

The words took a second to sink in. "You mean—?"

Shane slowly nodded. "Yeah. I'm buying Aimee a ring."

Now it was Aiden's turn to run his hand through his hair. "You mean, like get engaged? To be married? Have you thought this through? This is a huge commitment. Are you ready for that?"

Shane held up his hands. "Dude! Back off with all the questions. You sound like our sisters."

"Sorry," Aiden apologized. "You just caught me a little off guard here."

"Yeah, okay. But will you help me?"

Aiden placed his hand on his brother's shoulder. "I'm always here for you. But ring shopping? Don't you think you might have better success with Christel or Katie?"

"Uh, pass."

That made Aiden laugh. They both knew their sisters could be opinionated and were completely unafraid to push for their way of thinking. Katie was especially known for creating her own storms, only to cry when it rained."

Aiden paused, gathering up courage to speak what was really on his mind. "So, Shane. I'm not trying to be nosy. But, how are you going to pay for this ring?"

Shane shrugged off Aiden's concern. "I dipped into the money Dad left."

"Into your trust fund? Does Mom know?"

Shane again shrugged. "She would agree. I mean, Carson doesn't just need a mom and a dad. He needs a family. I need to step up and do the right thing here."

Aiden was shocked. Was this his little brother saying those things? "Well, yeah. That's a great outlook. And commendable. I still think you might want to stop and take a breath. Do you even love this girl?"

Shane leaned back against the hood of his car and folded his arms. "I don't only love this girl, I want to spend the rest of my life with her." He rubbed the back of his neck with his hand. "I haven't shared this with anyone until now, but I haven't wanted to be with anyone else since that day we met at Blackrock. I love everything about her." He let out a chuckle. "That's weird to hear coming out of my mouth, I know. Even to my ears. But it's true."

Aiden let out a low whistle. "I knew I shouldn't have gotten you that cologne sampler for Christmas."

Shane ignored him. "Seriously, Aiden. I was crushed when Aimee decided to leave for the mainland. I mean, I dealt with it because I didn't have a choice. Sometimes, fate or God, or whoever is up there pulling the strings—well, that person looks down and hands you some luck. It was awesome when Aimee showed back up at my door. Totally tubular! Carson was a surprise, but that tiny kid is *my* kid. That sealed the deal."

"So, Mom doesn't know at this point?"

"No, I'll tell her soon. I want to do this up epic...a surprise beach thing with rose petals or something. I saw that on an episode of *The Bachelorette* one time. I think girls dig those kinds of things."

"You watch the *The Bachelorette*?" Aiden deadpanned.

Shane ran a hand through his hair. "It's the weirdest thing. I turn it on and Carson goes right to sleep."

Aiden laughed. "Don't we all?"

Shane shrugged. "The girls are kinda hot."

"So, you sure you can support a family?" Aiden asked.

"I don't have a choice. Carson is my responsibility and I'll do whatever needs to be done to take care of him and Aimee."

Aiden stood there not knowing what to say. He liked to tease that in his little brother's case, alcohol was the liquid version of Photoshop. He'd party and any girl walking on two legs became worthy of attention. He woke up sleeping next to many of them the next morning...whether he knew their names or not. Hearing all these claims of love for Aimee now was a bit unnerving. There had been no transition. No gradual surrender into manhood. On second thought, that too was just like his brother. A wad of impulse on a surfboard.

"Well, Shane," Aiden said, shaking his head. "That's real mature of you. I only wish you a great future."

The jewelry store was located less than a half hour away. Aiden followed Shane in his car.

Inside, the shiny, tiled floor was lined with glass display cases filled with watches, necklaces, bracelets and rings. Bright lights positioned on the ceiling cast streams of light onto glittering colored gems and crystal, clear diamonds. Overhead music, the kind old people listened to, gently drifted from mounted speakers.

Shane immediately leaned over to Aiden. "Whew. Looks like this is the place."

A man lifted from where he sat examining a ring through a hand-held glass scope. He was balding and wore a pressed white shirt tightly buttoned over his paunch belly. "Good afternoon. Is there anything I can help you with?"

Aiden and Shane exchanged glances. Aiden nudged his brother.

"Uh, yeah. I need to buy a ring. An engagement ring."

The man lifted his chin slightly. "I see. Well, we have a nice selection to choose from. Do you have any particular budget in mind?"

Shane shook his head. "I—no, not really. I mean, I'm not terribly knowledgeable about what diamonds cost and all."

"I see." The man coughed and dug a jangling set of keys from his trousers. "Let me show you a few pieces in a range of budgets so you can get an idea of where you might land."

"Yeah, sure. That would be great." Shane gave the salesman a weak smile.

The salesman plucked several rings from the display case. He rolled out a spread of thick black velvet material onto the top of the display counter and placed the rings on the fabric, perfectly spaced. The bald gentleman motioned to the rings, from left to right, reciting the prices as he pointed.

Aiden winced. He hated when men got manicures.

Shane didn't hesitate. He picked the most expensive one and held it up to the light to examine his selection.

The salesman's eyes brightened. "Excellent taste, sir. That is a one and a quarter cushion cut solitaire of high cut and quality set in our highest-grade platinum—a show piece from our Blue Nile collection." He turned and quickly grabbed a companion piece from the case. "This is the matching wedding band. As you can see, the set is simply stunning. Your intended will be thrilled."

Shane nodded in agreement. "I'll take it."

Aiden nearly flipped. "Are you kidding? Look at how much that costs."

Shane stood firm. "Nope. I've made up my mind. I want Aimee to have that ring."

6

"Oh, my goodness! Are you kidding me?" Katie nearly dropped her weights.

Christel wiped her face with her gym towel. "Nope, our little brother bought Aimee a ring and is going to ask her to marry him."

"How do you know this?"

Christel unscrewed the lid on her water bottle. "He told Mom last night. Aiden went with him to pick it out. From what I'm told, it's gorgeous."

Katie flexed the hand weight toward her chest and out again. "Oh, that's rich. Two guys with no knowledge of jewelry trends or gem values walked into a jewelry store and bought an engagement ring. How much did it cost?"

"Well, I'm sure Mom thought it was rude to ask. But she did say he tapped into the money Dad left him to pay for it."

Katie's expression lifted as she let the weight drop to her side. "Whoa. How'd that go over? Mom must be completely undone about that."

"I don't think she was upset. I mean, I'm pretty sure she's happy he decided to commit to his son and his mother. I don't think she liked knowing they were simply camping out in the shanty together—her words, not mine." She let out a chuckle. "She said, and I quote: 'You can't run alongside your grown children with sunscreen and Chapstick. You have to let them live their lives and make their choices, good or bad.'"

"So, when is our little brother going to pop the question?"

Christel held up a forefinger while she took a drink from the bottle. Finished, she screwed the cap back on. "Soon. And that's where you and I come in. Apparently, he wants to make the proposal epic. Romantic. Mom says he wants us to help with that."

"Oh, now he wants our help." She grabbed Christel's water bottle out of her hand and unscrewed the cap.

"Hey, that's mine."

"So?" Katie ignored her sister's protest and took a drink from the bottle.

Christel scowled. "Hey, that's not exactly hygienic."

"Neither was sharing popsicles, Tootsie Pops and gum when we were little. Get over it." Katie handed the bottle back over, then the cap.

Christel huffed. "The least you could do is put the top back on."

Over the following days, Ava, Christel, and Katie teamed up to plan a grand proposal. From experience, each of them knew asking for your partner's hand in marriage was one of the biggest moments in your life. Special as it was, they wanted to ensure that the event was impressive and unforgettable.

After much back-and-forth, and a lot of internet research, Christel stumbled on the perfect way for their little brother to propose—a scavenger hunt ending up on the beach where Shane would bend to one knee, present the ring, and ask Aimee to be his wife.

"I love that," Katie exclaimed.

Their mother chimed in. "Me, too! It's romantic, creative, and full of fun. It's so Shane."

"Well, maybe not the romantic part, but certainly the element of fun fits our little brother," Christel told them.

"Oh, I think you've underestimated our little brother in the romance department. You saw that ring."

Finally, the big night arrived. The family gathered for pizza at Manoli's in Wailea. As the family chattered loudly around the large table, Shane quietly pushed a plate in front of Aimee with a slice of Hawaiian Honey—a thin-crusted pizza piled with honey smoked ham, caramelized pineapple, Maui onions, pomodoro sauce, and mozzarella. It was Aimee's favorite.

She held up her hands in protest. "Not another bite. I'm stuffed." That's when she saw the white note he had placed on top. "What's this?" she asked, pulling the small piece of paper closer so she could examine it.

The waiter, a stout man with a large belly covered by an apron, stepped to the table. "It is a family scavenger hunt," he announced.

"Yes," Ava confirmed, beaming. "I paid additional so we could have some extra fun tonight." She held up her phone. "And I'm going to record the entire thing with photos."

"A scavenger hunt?" Aimee asked.

"Just go with it," Shane told her. "Mom likes to do this stuff. We've learned not to argue."

"Be glad we're not bobbing for mangoes, like the last time," Katie said.

They all collectively groaned. "That was the worst," Willa stated emphatically. "You couldn't really bite into the thing, let alone lift it from the big bucket of water with your mouth."

Ava waved them off. "Okay, okay. Some of my ideas have been better than others, but this one is going to be fun. Read the clue, Aimee."

Aimee looked skeptical but obeyed. "It says, 'Go take a look where you'd go to buy a book. If you're going to be right, you'll search the shelves on the right. If you wish to know where from there, blue is your clue.'" She looked up puzzled. "I don't get it."

"The book store!" Christel and Katie shouted in unison.

Aiden grinned. "There's a book store in Wailea, isn't there?"

Ava nodded. "A Barnes and Noble. Let's go!"

Thankfully, Aimee bought off on the idea and seemed none the wiser as they paid the bill and raced to their cars. Minutes later, they blew through the front doors of the Barnes and Noble store.

"Shelves on the right," Shane reminded.

Ava and her family scrambled through the store in that direction. "Blue is the clue," Ava shouted.

They each worked hard at scouring the shelves, pulling any blue-spined book they could find. Disappointing groans signaled lack of success until Willa yelled, "Found it!"

She held a copy of *Under a Maui Sky* by Kellie Coates Gilbert in her hand and waved it over her head.

They all ran to join her. She reopened the front cover. Inside was another piece of paper. She gave it to her mom to read.

Katie cleared her throat. "You're finding clues and feeling bold. Now go to the place that keeps food really cold."

"They're kidding, right?" Aiden complained in jest. "Where's the closest grocery store?"

"It could be a convenience store," Christel suggested.

"Nah, I'm going with the big freezers at HoloHolo Market. Who's with me?" he asked.

They made the trek to the grocery store and hastened to the back of the store, to the frozen food aisle.

"This is going to be harder than I thought," Jon complained.

"Got it," Aimee yelled. "Look, there it is. Taped to a pint of peach ice cream." Her eyes beamed like a little kid at Christmas. "It says, 'If you want to find the next clue, go where the coffee is brewed.'"

Christel immediately alerted them to the fact that they'd passed a Starbucks only a block prior to turning into the store parking lot. They scrambled back to their cars and headed that way.

The next clue was handed to them by the barista. "I suppose you are looking for this."

Katie nodded. "Yes, we are. Thanks." She quickly opened the piece of paper and read the words out loud. "It's time to play in the sand. Makena Cove beach is where you should land. With any luck it will be found in a bucket.'"

In the car on the way, Aimee looked at Shane. "Okay, admittedly, I thought all this sounded a little lame. But it's kind of fun."

Shane leaned and brushed a kiss on her hand. "Mom is always the instigator of fun." He rolled his eyes as if he didn't quite agree with what he'd said.

Makena Cove was the closest beach. The early evening view was stunning. Even though Shane had seen it a bunch of times, he could never get over the cove's delicate size and sheer intimacy created by the lava croppings that bordered the stretch of sand. Or, how the sky was painted a mix of blue and orange at this time of day.

Shane reached for Aimee's hand, his heart beginning to beat wildly in his chest. Well, this is it, he thought. His insides were completely wired, but his mom and sisters had pulled this off. He couldn't think of a more romantic place than right here.

Soft waves glossing on shore created a calming soundtrack as he walked Aimee in the direction of the water.

"There it is!" she exclaimed, pointing. "The bucket." She looked over her shoulder. "Aren't you guys coming?"

They all shook their heads. "You two go ahead," Ava said, smiling. "We'll stay here."

Puzzled, Aimee looked back at Shane. "What's up with that? Why would they bail on the final clue? There might be a prize."

"Oh, yeah. There just might be a prize involved."

They approached the bucket. Suddenly, a circle of stringed lights came on, surrounding where they stood and illuminating the beach around them.

"What? What is this?" she said, glancing all around. Then she spotted the small velvet-covered box in the bucket. "Oh, my god!" Both her fists went to her mouth.

Shane reached and retrieved the tiny case. He wished his dad could see him now. Maybe he would finally be proud.

Almost unable to breathe, he folded to one knee. He swallowed and cleared his throat. "Aimee, if someone told me this time last year I'd be right here, right now—well, I'd tell them they were crazy. I was never thinking of getting married. That is, until I met you. That day we ran into each other at Blackrock —" He choked a little. "Well, you were fearless and beautiful, and I just knew you were somebody special. You did something to my heart that day."

Shane squeezed Aimee's hand. "When you showed up at my door with Carson, it should have terrified me. Truth is, I was pretty glad. The world is tighter without you in it with me, and whenever you are around it looks spacious. I want to share my space in this world with you. You, me, and Carson. A real fam." He paused again, embarrassed that his eyes had filled with tears. "Bottom line, Aimee, I, like—I love you. Will you be my wife?"

He quit breathing, waiting for her answer.

"Yes," she said simply. "Yes, I'll marry you."

Relieved and elated, he rose and slipped the ring from the box and onto her finger. The diamond in the center caught the light and sparkled. He hesitated, then slowly wrapped his arms around her waist and kissed her. Her lips were warm and moist. It was the best kiss ever!

Shane's heart lifted into his throat as he pulled back and met her gaze. Her face broke into a timid smile.

Aimee said yes!

His mom, his sisters, and his brother stood several yards away. He turned in their direction and pumped his fist in the air.

His family lowered their camera phones and cheered.

7

Ava woke to the sound of giggling girls. She smiled, grabbed her robe and made her way to the kitchen where Willa and her new friend, Kina, were sitting at the counter eating ice cream.

Ava chuckled. "Well, that looks like a healthy breakfast."

Willa grinned back at her grandmother. "It has milk," she argued.

Ava shot her granddaughter an amused look. "And a lot of sugar." She made her way to Willa and planted a kiss on her cheek. "Did you girls sleep well?"

Willa nodded enthusiastically. "Thanks for letting us stay here for our sleepover, Nana. Our house is so small right now. I can't wait until we get to move into the new one. Most especially because then Mom will quit stressing over every little detail. She's driving us all crazy. Especially Dad. I mean, who cares if the color of the flooring is chestnut or slate?" She let out a heavy sigh. "And that architect guy, Jasmit Tan, he's just weird. Mom is so impressed, though. If he said the house should be painted purple, Mom would clap her hands with delight and agree."

"Your mom is a bit...well, focused. I suppose we all need to have patience. This house means a lot to her." Maybe too much, Ava thought as she moved for the refrigerator. "Could I interest you girls in a second course...perhaps some eggs and bacon?"

Kina put her hand to her stomach. "Thank you, Mrs. Briscoe. But I couldn't eat anything more. We had a slice of pineapple upside down cake before Willa dished up the ice cream."

Ava groaned. "Goodness, don't tell your mother you are allowed to eat like this at my house. After she finishes scolding me, she'll surely limit visiting hours."

Willa laughed. "You got that right." She scooped her bowl clean with her spoon and put a final bite in her mouth. She rolled her eyes with pleasure. "I love the cherry chocolate flavor, Nana. You need to buy that kind all the time." She grabbed the empty bowls and walked them to the sink. "Maybe for the wedding? Last night was so romantic. Wasn't it, Nana? When I get engaged, I want something just like that." She rinsed the bowls and put them in the dishwasher. "Kina, you should have seen it. We did a family scavenger hunt that led to the beach where Uncle Shane got down on one knee and proposed. Aimee had no idea. He really surprised her."

Kina's eyes grew dreamy. "Ooh...that does sound romantic. When's the wedding?"

Ava poured herself a glass of juice. "They haven't set a date yet, but I suspect soon."

"Do you think they'll get married here at Pali Maui?" Kina asked. "I can't imagine a prettier place."

Willa returned to the counter. "Uncle Shane will be pushed to marry at Wailea Seaside Chapel. Nana's best friend's husband is the pastor. And no doubt, Alani will want to do a luau after, right Nana?"

Kina's interest was immediately piqued. "Alani...isn't that the lady who attended the retreat with you, Mrs. Briscoe?"

Ava leaned against the counter, juice glass in hand. "Yes," she confessed. "Alani has been a close friend of mine for years." She smiled and joined the girls at the island, standing across from where they sat. "By the way, Kina, your mother is lovely. We really enjoyed our time at the Banana Patch." Okay, that was a stretch. There were parts she did enjoy...like the massage. That said, she scratched bug bites for days after the fireside chanting.

"My mom's a little like Willa's. One track. For her, it's the Banana Patch," she admitted. "She eats, breathes, and sleeps thinking about that place. When she's not focused on the retreat center, she's chanting or doing yoga. Don't tell her, but I hate the smell of incense."

Ava laughed inside. She wasn't fond of that smoky scent, either. "So, how's school?" she asked, changing the subject.

Both girls shrugged at the same time. "It's okay," Willa answered. "Homework is really lame, like the teachers are really piling it on. I think there must be some secret contest to see who can assign the most."

Kina agreed. "I spent three hours last week on one assignment...an essay about how novels shape society."

Willa groaned. "Mrs. Johnson."

Kina nodded. "Yup."

Ava finished her juice and rinsed out the glass. "Willa, Christel tells me your friend is back." Ava tried to sound nonchalant when she asked the question. Christel had shared that the girl was no longer pregnant, causing Katie to voice great reservation about the influence that girl had over Willa. Ava had to agree. She turned and moved to the sink, grabbed a wet rag, and wiped the counter. "Now, what was her name?" she asked over her shoulder, again trying to avoid looking like she was fishing for information.

"Do you mean Amanda? Yeah, she's back," Willa answered. "Not that that's a good thing."

Ava turned to face the girls and lifted her brows. "Oh? Why's that?"

Kina quickly answered, "She's kind of bossy." When Ava looked surprised, Kina added, "Over the top. Sometimes she's mean."

Ava moved to the island and continued wiping. "Oh?" she prodded.

Willa turned to her friend. "Look, like I told you, don't put up with her. She gets all salty if people don't bow to her every whim. I know from experience." She shook her head. "Just avoid her."

Ava was glad to hear that. Sounded like Katie might not have as much to worry about as earlier thought.

Kina swiveled her stool back and forth. "It's not always so easy to just ignore Amanda and those girls who hang with her."

Ava grew concerned. "Why do you say that? Honey, did something happen?"

Kina shrugged. "Amanda's in my science class and when the teacher was called out of the room for a moment, she stood and announced to the entire class that I was homeless and ate at the shelter. Worse? She called my mom a 'jungle-slut.'"

"What?" Willa demanded. "You're kidding me. Why didn't you tell me?"

Again, Kina shrugged. "I didn't want to make it worse, so I just ignored it."

Ava's hand went to her chest. "Oh, honey. That's awful. That girl's mother needs to be alerted that her daughter is saying those dreadful things."

Kina put up open palms. "No, please. I don't think that's a good idea."

Willa shook her head in agreement. "Yeah, that lady wouldn't win any Mother of the Year awards. I'm not sure she'd even care. When Amanda got pregnant, her mom completely wigged out worrying about how it would look. She whisked her off and fixed the problem."

Ava tried not to blanch at the words, "fixed the problem." Were these girls mature enough to understand what they were talking about? And to say it so flippantly. Still, it was a different time than when Ava grew up. She chose to not lecture and instead took a deep breath and parked her hands on her hips. "I hate to say it, but that girl sounds like a bully. You might be right about not talking to her mother. I wouldn't want to make things worse. Even so, something needs to be done."

That something, she decided, was to make sure Katie and Jon were aware of this bullying issue.

Later that night, she expressed her concern to her daughter.

"She's a troublemaker," Katie declared, upon learning of the situation.

Jon agreed. "Yeah, obviously I'm not too keen on the fact she took a pregnancy test in our house and tossed it in the garbage for me to find. Caused more than a few problems."

"All that aside, I really do not like mean girls," Katie added.

"Do you think you should bring this up with her mother? Perhaps let her nip this behavior in the bud?" Ava suggested. She told them what the girls had said about Amanda's mother.

"Well, that might be so, but I still think it's a good idea to go to her parents," Jon said.

"I'm not sure Amanda's dad is currently in the picture. Regardless, you're both right. We should go pay Mrs. Cooper a visit."

"We?" Jon asked, lobbing her with a look of surprise. "Don't you think this is a woman-to-woman kind of discussion?"

Katie rolled her eyes and huffed. "Oh, fine. I'll go talk to her."

Ava learned that Katie intended to address this immediately and planned to go the following day. Unfortunately, Ava's phone rang bright and early the next morning.

"Mom! Noelle has a bright red rash all over her stomach and down one arm. Can you come take a look?"

Ava promised she would and headed right over. One of the beauties of living so close is that the walk took only minutes. She knocked on her daughter's door.

The door flung open. "Come look. Seriously, Mom...the rash is awful."

When Katie lifted her little daughter's shirt, Ava bent for a closer look and examined her red, angry flesh. "Could be a number of things, but it's obvious the poor baby is itching." As if on cue, Noelle started howling.

Katie scooped her up. "Well, I'm just going to take her to the pediatrician."

"Give me a minute and I'll go grab my purse and go with you." Katie tended to become overly anxious when it came to her children being sick. "I'll alert Christel and tell her that we'll both be gone for a few hours, just in case anything comes up."

Katie nodded and voiced her appreciation. "I'll call Jon."

Their family pediatrician, Dr. Stein, was located in the same office building as Dr. Matisse with his door down the hall from Evan's. The aging physician had been the Briscoe kids' doctor ever since Christel put a tiny piece of coconut shell up her nose and got it stuck. Now, he was caring for Jon and Katie's children.

Dr. Stein settled his wire-rim glasses on his nose and leaned over little Noelle's body on the examination table. "Ah...uh-huh," he murmured. He lifted Noelle's arm to take a closer look.

She looked back at him with her bottom lip quivering, as if she might break out crying again at any moment.

"Oh...yes. Uh-huh," he repeated. He straightened. "Wait here a moment. I'll be right back." He turned and left the office.

Katie's face grew even more worried. "This doesn't look good," she said, nervously patting her leg.

"Now, let's not borrow trouble," Ava warned. "It's a rash, Katie. Not cancer."

"But, you and I both know—"

Before she could finish her sentence, Dr. Stein returned to the room with a handheld magnifier. In the other hand, he held a lollipop. Grinning, he said, "This is to keep the patient still." He winked.

He examined Noelle's rash for several minutes. When finished, he took a deep breath and turned to face Katie. "Well, what we have here is a case of mites."

"Mites!" Katie nearly screamed. "Noelle has mites?"

Dr. Stein chuckled. "It's more common than you think."

Katie burst into tears. "But I keep my children clean," she lamented.

Ava put her arm around her daughter. "Oh, honey. This has nothing to do with your hygiene practices. It happens. Trust me. Both Aiden and Shane got hair lice once." She turned to Dr. Stein. "Remember?"

He smiled and nodded. "Yes, I remember." He folded the magnifier and slipped it into the pocket of his white coat. "Do you have dogs?"

Katie sniffed. "Yes. Givey."

"Has the pup been scratching excessively? Your daughter may have held the dog in her arms and the mites migrated. If so, you'll need to arrange a visit to the vet as soon as possible."

Katie shook her head. "I haven't noticed Givey scratching." Suddenly, her eyes widened. "Can you get mites from roosters? I did catch her carrying a rooster through the yard yesterday." She turned to Ava. "I made her put the thing right down. I was so surprised it didn't peck her."

"We have lots of wild roosters that wander through the grounds at Pali Maui," Ava explained to Dr. Stein.

"Well, that's likely the culprit," he agreed. "Either way, here's some cream to rid Noelle of the problem." He reached in his other pocket and offered a small tube. "This sample should be enough. If not, I'll write a prescription. Apply this liberally, not only the areas where the rash appears, but over her entire body. Leave it on for at least twelve hours."

Katie rubbed her forehead, clearly upset. "Thank you, Dr. Stein. Is the rest of the family in danger of getting this rash?"

The minute her daughter said this, Ava felt her skin crawl.

Dr. Stein shook his head. "It's not likely. Only in rare cases can mites be transmitted from human to human. These are simple poultry mites. If it would make you feel better about the situation, simply wash her bedding and clothing in extremely hot water."

Both Ava and Katie released a grateful sigh. They thanked Dr. Stein profusely, then they gathered up Noelle and the cream, and headed home.

The day had taken a definite twist from how Ava planned to spend her time. Tomorrow, she'd have to make up for the lost work hours. Perhaps skip lunch and have dinner brought over to her.

Still, it gave Ava great comfort knowing she was available and could drop everything any time one of her children needed her. Problems were easier to face with someone by your side.

Only when Ava climbed in bed that night did she realize one important problem still remained. In the havoc, Amanda Cooper's bullying got shoved aside.

8

Katie pulled the wet load of laundry from the washer and shoved the items into the dryer. "Jon! Are the girls ready? They need to eat breakfast before we leave," she hollered.

Just once, she wished she didn't have to act as her husband's caretaker. It was as if she were his walking calendar, set with reminders so Jon didn't miss all the events in his life—both big and small. In business, he was a master at juggling a lot of balls. In his personal life, everything seemed to fall to her. "Jon, did you hear me?"

Her husband yelled back from the kitchen. "Yes, Katie. You don't have to yell. I heard." She could hear him slam the refrigerator door. "Look, I need to run. I'm meeting a new supplier, the one from Idaho with the morel mushrooms. I've been on his waiting list for over a year. He's in Maui on vacation and graciously agreed to take time away from his family to connect."

Katie huffed and headed for the living room. Jon already had his hand on the doorknob. "Well, Jasmit and I are at a critical juncture. We have to make some decisions on the lighting for the master bathroom. We're extremely fortunate Jasmit has extended his expertise and is willing to babysit every step, even to the point of assisting me in making design choices."

Jon shook his head. "You're kidding, right? Another meeting on the house? They're never ending. What more could you possibly have to pick out?"

Katie lifted her chin. "The fact that you don't know the answer to that reveals you have no clue what goes into creating a residential masterpiece. Did you even listen when I said Jasmit thinks our house will be featured on Architectural Design website as one of the top ten builds of the year? Architectural Design, Jon. That's a huge deal." Katie gave him a pointed look. "There's canister lighting, wall sconces, well-placed table lamps. Each one gives a very different look. The lighting is critical."

Jon lifted open hands and folded. "Fine!" He quickly paced down the hallway and parked himself in front of the girls' shared bedroom. "Willa! Move it," he hollered through the closed door.

Satisfied with her win, Katie headed for the shower. She had less than an hour before her meeting.

The prize-winning architect arrived right on time. He stepped out of a shiny silver sports car wearing a casual button-down shirt open halfway to his navel and sunglasses pushed up in his messy, jet-black hair, and headed in her direction.

A buzzy feeling ran across Katie's stomach when she saw rolled-up building plans tucked under his arm and a pile of glossy sales brochures in his other hand. She was in her element. Designing and building this house had been her joy, the thing that filled her up. Sure, she had responsibilities at Pali Maui. She managed the giftshop and the tours. Frankly, she could run those in her sleep. This—well, this project had given her a reason to wake each morning.

Much of that could be attributed to Jasmit Tan. His accolades were well-known in the architectural world. She and Jon were indeed fortunate when he agreed to work with them on their new home.

His designs focused on harmony between building and site. Each project sought a poetic experience of its location—a view over a pool seamless with the ocean; a second-story open-air porch that hung among tree branches; a city apartment and roof deck from which one saw moving columns of light on asphalt in the rain.

Like she, Jasmit had a vision for her new home. Every detail mattered. Every color choice. Every fixture. All of it contributed to the look they were going for. This was her dream home, her sanctuary. Nothing was subject to abatement. No expense was spared. Jon would throw a fit if he knew exactly how much some of this cost. Some things were better left undisclosed.

"Good morning, Katie," Jasmit called out as he neared. "Are you ready to get to work?"

Katie lifted on her toes and looked past him. "Is that a new car?"

The Johnny Depp look-alike grinned. "It is. A Bentley Bacalar I had shipped over from Germany."

"From Germany?" Her gut clenched a bit at the thought. Not only did that car cost more than Jon would make in a lifetime, shipping overseas carried a tremendous price tag. According to Mom and Christel, transport shipping was one of Pali Maui's top expense items.

As if reading her mind, he was quick to add, "While it may seem outrageous to spend that kind of money, I've decided to remain in Maui—" He paused. "Long term." His chiseled face broke into a measured smile, waiting for her reaction.

Katie's eyebrows lifted. "Well, that is a surprise."

She knew he'd recently moved to the island from Singapore, but she expected his stay would be temporary. The internet sites said he moved often. He'd lived in Nice, France before a small stint in a little hamlet in Switzerland. From there, he stayed in Bolivia for a time. Then Taiwan. That wasn't counting all the places he'd vacationed. There were plenty of photos of the exotic places where he'd traveled. Often, he had a beautiful woman on his arm. Now, he was making his home in Maui?

"Regardless, welcome. You are now officially one of us," she told him, secretly glad. Perhaps they could work on another project—possibly a renovation of the golf clubhouse here on Pali Maui—a project she'd recently championed to her mom and sister. Would Jasmit even take on a project that small? Especially since he was in such demand?

He followed her up a flight of steps and across a wraparound deck to the door of her nearly finished home. Inside, everything was coming together. It looked even better than she'd hoped.

"Let me show you something." Jasmit moved to the massive kitchen island and rolled out one of the plans he'd carried in. "I think we should incorporate a steam shower into the fixtures. This feature is all the rage in Europe. The installation would only push back completion by a day or so."

Katie quickly warmed to the idea. Jon would love to steam after a long day at the restaurant. "What would be the added cost?"

Jasmit recited an amount that made Katie swallow...hard.

"Oh, I'm not sure—"

"I could offer the shower fixture at my cost, a substantial discount from retail. You'd still have to pay labor, of course. I strongly urge you to consider the addition. The increased value of this home would pay for the investment."

Katie carefully considered what he said. On the downside, that argument had been the same when she'd stretched and included the curved ceiling, placed warmers under the tile so the flooring would not be chilly in the mornings, and when she'd agreed to the hand-hammered copper freestanding oval tub. The cost of that little puppy added over thirteen-thousand to the price tag of this master bath, but—oh, that patina on the metal!

    She was out of control. Somewhere on the inside, she knew it. Her mind kept warning, "No!" But her mouth said, "Yes, yes, yes."

Then there was the kitchen—the forty-eight-inch built-in refrigerator with French doors that perfectly matched the cabinets, the wine cooler and the coffee bar with built-in expresso and frothing machines. All that had cost a pretty penny. She hadn't meant to go over budget, but like Jasmit had reminded on several occasions, it was much less expensive to incorporate into the original design than to add these features later, if she even could.

"So, are we going to include the steamer shower?" Jasmit asked. Those nearly black eyes drilled in on her, waiting.

She tried to breath normally. No, definitely not. She was already over budget.

"Yes," she nodded. "I think Jon would like that." Okay, in her head, she was desperately grasping at justification for another overage on what they'd planned to spend, but she'd gotten her tub. The least she could do was to add something for her husband.

Jasmit's face broke into an enthusiastic grin. "Excellent!"

9

Christel climbed from Evan's Jeep and knelt to tie her sneakers a little tighter. "This was such a good idea," she said as she straightened. "I haven't been hiking for months."

"I'm looking forward to it to," he said. "Hope this wasn't too early for you."

"No, not at all. I love early mornings."

They'd chosen the Waihe'e Ridge Trail, a five-mile round trip hike with smashing valley views and a winding path through a vigorous forest of guava, kukui, swamp mahogany, and Cook Island pines. With the trail gaining about fifteen hundred feet at the pinnacle, most trekkers started no later than eight in the morning to avoid the clouds that inevitably rolled in later in the morning, diminishing the view.

They walked about five hundred feet in blissful silence, taking in the beauty of their surroundings, when Evan turned to Christel. "So, I want to know more about the big proposal."

Christel smiled and spilled the details of how the Briscoe family had gone out for pizza, then participated in a scavenger hunt. The final clue led them to Makena Cove.

"I love that beach," Evan said. "I think it's the way the stretch of sand is bordered on either side by lava rock croppings. Gives an epic...and yet intimate feel."

"Yes, it was the perfect place for a wedding proposal." She explained how surprised Aimee was when she discovered the rest of the family hung back and Shane took her hand and led her to a bucket perched out in the sand. As they neared, Uncle Jack flipped a switch and a circle of tiny white lights illuminated the area. "Uncle Jack and Aiden went out ahead of time and set everything up. They buried a lengthy electric cord beneath the sand. When it was time, a battery-operated power source did the trick."

"Clever," Evan commented. "I don't think I'd have thought of all that."

Christel felt her heart rate pick up as the path grew more steep. "Uncle Jack can build anything, fix anything, and tinkers until he finds a way to jury-rig any contraption—even magical lighting on a remote beach."

Evan laughed. "Good to know." He took the towel draped around his neck and wiped his brow. "So, when's the wedding?"

"I'm not sure. What I am sure of is that there's a little tension building. Shane and Aimee are considering something simple, perhaps on that same beach with Uncle Jack officiating. He's allowed as a boat captain and a licensed wedding officiant."

"So, what's the problem?"

"Mom is urging him to reconsider and hold a more traditional ceremony at Wailea Chapel. While she acknowledges it is Shane and Aimee's decision, she's hoping Elta will marry them. I think she's afraid her best friend, Alani, will be hurt otherwise."

"Ah, yes. I see the problem."

"Mom will back off, of course. She's not one to push and

push. She's much more subtle. She's so gracious about not taking her advice or recommendation that you feel guilty."

They both laughed.

"No matter what the final decision ends up being, you'll be my 'plus one.' You will come with me to my little brother's wedding?" She knew a surgeon's schedule was never carved in stone. Evan could easily get called for an emergency. She'd certainly understand. When he'd cared for Shane, she was extremely grateful for his attention.

"I'd like that. I don't often admit this, but I love wedding cake. The bigger, the better. And all flavors, though I love strawberry champagne with buttercream frosting the best."

Christel burst out laughing in spite of herself. "Really? Evan, you are filled with surprises." She turned and looked at him in wonder. "You are the most interesting man I've ever met. Truly."

"So, you think we're good together?"

"Epic," she said, smiling.

They rounded a bend in the trail. "Whether my brother weds on the beach or in a chapel, there will be cake. I can promise you that."

They entered a portion of the trail that was canopied with trees and foliage. Long strands of moss hung from limbs several feet up in the air. Christel was reminded of a scene in the *Wizard of Oz*, when Dorothy and her companions entered the haunted forest. Those images still creeped her out, even as an adult. Just like this portion of the trail.

Her only hope was knowing this dreadful dark didn't last long.

Several switchbacks just ahead led to the crest of a hill known as Lani-Lani. There, a small wooden deck with a picnic table would be waiting. The views were grand from that location.

Christel picked up the pace, hoping to exit this portion of

the trail as quickly as possible. Evan was close behind, whistling a tune made popular by Green Day—"Time of Your Life." Another thing they had in common. Growing up, she had all their recordings, and played them often.

Suddenly, her foot slipped on a pebble. Before she could catch herself, she went down and her ankle turned, sending a bolt of pain shooting up her leg.

Evan rushed to her side. "Christel, are you okay?" His voice was filled with concern, especially when Christel's eyes teared up.

He threw off his jacket. "Don't move," he ordered. "It may be broken."

She almost laughed, and would, if the pain wasn't so severe. How handy to fall and break your leg with an orthopedic surgeon by your side.

Evan carefully maneuvered her into a position where he could examine her injury. He removed her sneaker and sock and looked at her ankle. It was already swollen to nearly twice its normal size and was turning a very unhealthy shade of purple. His fingers gently probed and pressed, ever so slightly.

Christel grimaced and tried her best not to protest.

He finally looked up. "Well, we won't know if it's broken until we get an x-ray."

"Broken?" Christel teared up even more at the idea of a fracture. Worse? How would she possibly get off this mountain with an injured ankle? The swelling and intense pain signaled she certainly wouldn't be walking back to the car.

She looked over at Evan and groaned miserably. "What a mess. I can't believe I did this." Her voice betrayed the calm she was now trying to portray.

"Accidents happen," he said. "Believe me, I often see much worse. We just need to get you back to the car and to the ER so I can get those x-rays." He assured her everything would be fine. He had a plan.

Evan warned her to try not to move that ankle. He bent and scooped his arms under her knees and around her back, positioning his hands to keep her steady.

Christel turned horrified. "Evan, no! You can't carry me. I'm too heavy."

He closed his eyes and smiled. "You let me be the judge of that." He lifted her from the ground, the effort appearing far easier for him than she estimated it would be.

"You're allowed to grunt. I won't take offense," she teased, even though the movement caused her to wince.

Suddenly, they heard thunder. "Oh no," Christel moaned as she craned her neck for a look at the sky. Anyone who spent much time on Maui knew brief rain showers were typical in the higher elevations, hence the thick, green foliage. Thunder and lightning were rare and often signaled a torrential downpour was on the way. Storms like this could appear out of nowhere, carried in by warm trade winds.

"Looks like we'd best get moving," Evan said. As an afterthought, he added, "I have a first aid kit in the car."

Before the words were out of his mouth, the first drops fell. Big ones pelting the ground with force and coming at a quickly increasing rate. They both knew that at any moment, the sky would open and they would get soaked.

Evan picked up the pace and jogged until he reached the place on the trail covered with the canopy of trees. The limbs and thick foliage would provide protection to some extent.

"Over there." Christel nodded toward a location tucked near a large boulder bordered with large ferns, where the ground was mossy. Overhead, dense, closely-packed strawberry guava limbs helped complete the shelter.

Evan hurried to the spot. He ducked and gently placed Christel near the rock. "You good?" he asked, looking concerned.

She nodded. "I'd be better if I could walk and you didn't

have to carry me out of here." The initial pain had subsided but was replaced with a throbbing that made her eyes water.

Another crack of thunder rang out, startling both of them. Large droplets quickly followed, pounding the ground outside their makeshift shelter.

"Are you comfortable? I mean, notwithstanding that angry ankle." He settled himself into a spot next to her. "Are you cold?" Without waiting for her response, he slid his arm around her and pulled her close.

Christel sighed and leaned against his shoulder, appreciating his strong muscles and the way he smelled. It had been a long, long time since a man had taken care of her. She was so used to playing custodian over Jay's life, she'd nearly forgotten how it felt to lean on a man for support, knowing he would be there for her.

Emotion clotted her throat. Evan was smart and strong and dependable. There was no mistaking he cared deeply for her. She felt the same.

Christel curled up next to him, traced her fingers down his strong forearm. He responded by silently lifting her chin and kissing her so gently, she filled with wonder.

She let her eyes drift closed and listened to the rain, trying to absorb this moment, wrap herself in it like a warm blanket.

Loving Jay was like flying—adventurous flying without taking a breath—through the air, weightless. Reckless. From early on, he consumed her and never let go. In the end, he'd ripped her soul into tiny bits.

Evan had glued her back together.

She was safe.

10

Ava drove the utility terrain vehicle down the lane. Last night's rain, coupled with heavy semi-truck traffic, had created more than a few potholes. She gripped the steering wheel tighter as she jostled back and forth. She neared the packing shed and pulled to a stop, then killed the engine. "Hey, Mig." She waved at Miguel Nakamoto, the farm manager at Pali Maui.

Mig was nearly a fixture at Pali Maui, having worked at the pineapple plantation longer than anyone—nearly as long as Ava. His responsibilities included managing the fields and the packing operation and supervising the employees. He was good at his job and highly respected. Ava was grateful to work alongside him, especially now that her husband was gone.

"Well, well...is that a new UTV, Miss Ava?" he asked, grinning.

"It's for you," she announced, grinning. "We couldn't have you driving your classic down these bumpy roads, now, could we?" she teased, knowing he would never drive his baby down the plantation roads or in the pineapple fields.

Mig was extremely proud of his red and white 1955 Chevy

Bel Air, decked with wide white sidewall tires and rear wheel skirts. Everyone knew how much that car meant to him.

Mig laughed. "No, my Bel Air does not go off-road," he agreed.

Ava climbed from the UTV. "Well, Christel said we needed to use up some cash before the end of our fiscal year, for tax purposes. So, I thought I'd surprise you." His old UTV had blown a head gasket last week. They had a choice of paying for expensive repairs or investing in a new unit.

"Whoo-eee! She's a beaut," he said, whistling his appreciation. Mig walked around the farm vehicle, inspecting and admiring it.

Ava smiled and handed him the keys. "Did the shipment of sealer wax come in?

He nodded. "Yesterday."

"Good," she said as she followed him inside the packing shed. "I put a rush on it. Unfortunately, we're running against some shipping backlog from the mainland."

Mig hung his baseball cap on a peg and both he and Ava donned disposable hair caps before moving for the conveyers. Workers picked pineapples off the moving belt and placed them in cardboard shipping boxes.

While the pineapple harvest ran year-round, the heavy fruiting season ran primarily from March until June. It took two to three years for a single pineapple to reach maturation. This meant Pali Maui had to run like a well-oiled machine. Mig was a big part of making that happen. That did not mean that Ava was hands-off. She helped direct the planting and harvesting.

Lincoln often criticized and said her oversight was unnecessary. She disagreed.

After Lincoln passed away, she heard the rumors. Gossip went around suggesting she wasn't up for running the entire operation without her husband. Little did they know she had always run this operation. Lincoln was only the masthead.

When they'd finished looking over the packing effort, Mig followed Ava outside. "So, I hear Shane popped the question."

Ava broke into a wide smile. "Yes, and Aimee said yes."

Mig laughed. "Does this gal know what she's in for?"

"Do any of us know what to expect when we marry?" Ava countered.

The farm manager's deep-brown skin crinkled at the eyes as he laughed again. "No." He shook his head. "I don't suppose we do." Mig had been divorced for nearly a decade. His ex-wife was known as the "plate thrower."

They walked in the direction of the fields. A tour bus filled with visitors slowly passed, speakers blaring. "Pali Maui is self-sufficient, even down to the fuel used in the trucks. The seeds from those sunflowers along the river are harvested and used to make biodiesel."

Ava and Mig exchanged glances. This is where fascinated tourists threw their hands up with questions—all of which would be answered by the bus driver as the bus leaned around the tight corner and headed for the first field.

"How is Christel?" Mig asked.

"She really did a number on her ankle," Ava answered. "It wasn't broken, but she sure sprained it good. But you know Christel. She never missed a minute of work. She simply propped the wrapped ankle up on an empty printer box and soldiered on." Ava stepped over a dip in the roadway that was filled with muddy water. "What do you hear from your daughter, Mig?"

"Leilani is a good girl. She calls me every week even though she's very busy. Her PR firm recently landed a contract with a big-selling romance author who lives in Seattle." Mig kicked a rotting pineapple off the road with the toe of his boot. "Who knew those romance authors made that much money?"

"Yeah?"

"Oh, yes. Leilani says bare man chests really sell." He broke into his signature laughter.

"Maybe that's your problem, Mig. You keep your shirt buttoned up," she teased.

Mig was quick to wave her off. "Ay, ay, ay...that field's been harvested long ago. I'm not about to replant it."

Ava reached her arm around her farm manager and gave him a little hug. "I'm right there with you, friend."

11

Shane quickly tethered the dock line to the tie down on the starboard side of his uncle's boat, then moved to the port side and did the same. When he'd finished mooring, he climbed aboard and raced for his pack, then jumped back onto the dock.

"What are you in an all-fire hurry for, boy?" Captain Jack asked while chewing on his cigar. He rubbed his generous belly and laughed. "You already caught that girl. No need for running like a lovelorn chicken with your head cut off now."

Shane hesitated as to whether he wanted to reveal his motives. His upcoming appointment wasn't a secret, but he didn't have time to counter any push back.

His uncle sensed his reluctance and spit into the water. "Spill it, boy."

Shane swallowed. "I—I'm meeting a realtor and I'm going to be late."

"A realtor?" His uncle's bushy eyebrows shot up. "You selling a house?"

"Buying one," Shane told him. "Look, I really gotta go." Before Uncle Jack could pummel him with any more questions,

Shane took off running toward the Banyan tree. "See you tomorrow," he called back over his shoulder.

He jogged easily across the small park and down the sidewalk to where he'd parked knowing that he was going to take a lot of flak from his family when they learned of his decision. They'd say he should hold back on taking on a mortgage until he and Aimee had been married at least a year.

His mother would remind him the shanty where they currently lived was small, but it was free.

Christel would warn that buying a house was a complicated matter, that he couldn't just jump into something of this financial magnitude without careful thought and planning...and a lot of help from someone who could guide him—someone who understood loan rates and amortization schedules. Of course, his sister was a CPA and everything was a spreadsheet to her.

When Aiden heard, he would shake his head thinking his little brother had jumped off Black Rock and hit his head.

Not everyone would be critical. Aunt Vanessa would play the cheerleader and say, "Good for you!" His sister Katie, would be delighted and want to help him decorate and his friends would be like, "Cool, we'll have a place to crash."

Shane reached his car and unlocked the door. Didn't matter. The only opinion that mattered to him was that of his fiancee's.

Shane climbed into his car and started the engine, not entirely sure what Aimee would say when she learned of his plan. Once he had worked with a realtor and was sure he could qualify for the mortgage, he'd spring the idea on her. She might panic at first, but then he'd reveal that the remaining money his dad had left in trust gave them options. They weren't stuck raising Carson in that tiny place near his mom, even if it was free. Aimee and his kid deserved better, and he was going to give it to them.

The new house wouldn't be a fixer-upper, either. Aiden may

enjoy renovating over many months. He'd been at the process for over a year and his house in Lahaina was still a dump.

No, he was going to impress Aimee with a place she'd always wanted. A place she could easily call home.

Shane had found his realtor on a social media site. From what he'd read, Wimberly Ann Jenkins had just relocated to the island from a little town in Arkansas and had brought her wealth of real estate experience with her. The post didn't say what that experience entailed, but there were a ton of likes. The likes were mostly from men and might not be associated with her skill as a realtor, but rather the fact her lady bumps were pretty substantial. Still, Shane thought she looked professional. When they'd talked on the phone, she seemed to know her stuff and assured him he'd be in good hands.

The realtor showed up a few minutes late. She strolled into the open-air lobby of the Hyatt wearing a hot pink suit and matching stiletto heels that clacked loudly as she made her way across the shiny tile floor. Her blonde hair was shoulder-length and reminded Shane of a vintage Hollywood bombshell, the way her hair was curled to dip over one eye, just so.

When she spotted him, she waved and blew him a kiss. "Oh, honey, I hope I didn't keep you waiting long," she told him, looking a little flustered. "I mistakenly went to the Hyatt Residence next door before I realized I was in the wrong place and was supposed to meet you at the Hyatt Regency." She flung her hair off her shoulder.

Yeah, she was definitely the glamour type, he thought, as they made introductions and shook hands. Wimberly Ann was probably fifty-ish, trying to look like she was in her thirties—the kind of female who spent a lot of time in front of the mirror and spent considerable amounts of money on face stuff.

"Don't worry. That happens a lot," he told her.

Wimberly Ann rolled her eyes. "Well, they should change the name, or something. It's really confusing."

She lowered into a plush armchair and immediately unloaded her briefcase, positioning small stacks of papers side-by-side on the low lobby table before them. "I just thought I'd bring a few things for you to look at," she explained.

Suddenly, she stopped her activity.

"Oh, my. Isn't that a pretty sight?" She motioned to the outer courtyard, a picture-book tropical paradise with tall palms swaying alongside pools and waterfalls. "I have to pinch myself nearly every day, hardly able to believe I really live in Maui." She nearly giggled. "I mean, who gets this lucky?"

Shane leaned and pointed to the documents on the table. "Uh, I don't know much about buying houses. That looks like a lot of information."

"Oh, honey. It's not really. I took the information you gave me over the phone and got you a preliminary loan approval. Of course, that approval is subject to a lot of things before they give the final okay. Still, it's enough for you to move forward with confidence," she advised.

Wimberly picked up another stack and held them out to him. "These are some options I think you should consider. All are in your price range, and in Lahaina, like you requested."

She watched him expectantly as he examined the listing sheets. Finally, he looked up. "Yeah, there's a lot I like here."

Wimberly clapped her hands. "Oh, good. I was hoping you'd say that, honey." She pulled her phone from her bag. "Let me make some calls and line up some showings. This afternoon good?"

Shane nodded enthusiastically. "Yeah, sure." His plan was to narrow the selections down to two or three and then surprise Aimee with the news. From there, they could go look together and he'd let her choose her favorite.

The first house they looked at was north of downtown Lahaina in an area known as Napila-Honokowai. "This is a nice little three bedroom, two bath in a gated neighborhood. Schools are good and grocery stores nearby."

"I like the sound of that," he told her.

He liked the house very much, as well as the others Wimberly Ann showed him. There were two-stories, ranch-style, and even one with a peek of ocean view. His realtor seemed even more excited than him. "Oh, look at that bathroom!" she said clapping her hands. She stroked one of the counters. "I've always wanted a marble countertop just like this."

Over the afternoon, and with Wimberly Ann's help, Shane narrowed his choices down to three.

"Excellent," she said, locking up the last house on the schedule. "I'll pull additional information and put together packets for you on each of those houses." They made arrangements to meet again, after Shane revealed his plans to Aimee.

"Thank you," Shane told her as they walked to their cars.

"No, I'm the one who needs to thank you!" Wimberly Ann straightened her skirt, beaming back at him. "You're my first client here on Maui," she confided. "It's been a real pleasure. That fiancée of yours...well, she's one lucky gal." She sighed. "You can't beat true love. I'm a sucker for weddings. I've had six husbands."

Shane couldn't hide his surprise. "Six?"

"Oh, yes, honey. And I loved every one of them."

Shane didn't know about that. Six husbands were a lot, by anyone's measure. Personally, he planned to stick with just one wife.

Shane and Wimberly Ann parted ways, and Shane headed for his car.

He knew the statistics. Seemed like everywhere he turned, people were folding up their wedding vows and moving on. Heck, his own father had strayed and betrayed his family.

Shane unlocked the car door, thinking about how this time

last year, he'd have laughed if anyone told him he'd be engaged and shopping for houses. He'd have told them they were crazy. But that was before he lost his heart to Aimee and Carson.

Aimee was nothing like any of the other girls he'd hooked up with. She was smart. She was funny. She was amazing.

She was *his*.

Their marriage would last forever.

12

Katie climbed from her car, dropped her keys into her purse and headed for the front door of the shanty. This coming weekend, they'd be moving into their new house. Thanks to Jasmit Tan, the construction crew had finished ahead of schedule—and none too early. This tiny place was getting smaller by the day.

She hummed as she headed for the front door, deliriously happy with the way the house had turned out. The final build was everything she'd hoped for—open concept, lots of natural lighting, a massive kitchen island and high-end appliances. The master suite and bath were to die for!

She reached for the doorknob when suddenly the door opened. Jon stood inside, his fist clenched around some papers. He waved them in her face. "Do you want to explain why this says we are forty percent over budget?" His face was red.

Katie's heart leaped into her throat. She'd meant to put the house papers in her bedside drawer, intending on easing Jon into a discussion about how much she'd spent. First, she'd tell him about all the fantastic deals that were extended, compliments of the once-in-a-lifetime discounts Jasmit had arranged.

How could she possibly pass on opportunities to have Cristal Brut champagne for grocery store sparkling wine prices? Okay, maybe Dom Perignon.

Katie moved past her husband and placed her bag on the butcher block kitchen counter before turning to face his anger. She drew a tentative breath that was laced with equal parts of confidence and trepidation. "Jon, let me explain," she said, not liking what she saw in her husband's eyes. "If you understand the whole picture, I think you'll calm down and see those expenditures were not only warranted, they were great investments."

Jon's eyes widened. "Investments? What planet do you live on, Katie? The overage is equal to two years of my restaurant profits—two years!" He shook his head. "Do you have any concept of what this means? Besides that, you know we can never sell. That was part of the stipulation your mother placed on the deal when she gifted us land here at Pali Maui."

"Okay, okay...I hear you." Katie squared her shoulders. "I think you're overreacting. Jasmit said—"

"I don't care what Pretty-Boy said. For months, it's been Jasmit this. Jasmit that. He thinks this. He advises that." Her husband, who rarely lost his temper, scowled.

He tossed the papers on the counter. "Does it matter what your husband thinks? Did you ever stop to consider I needed to have a say in all this? We're a team, remember?"

Katie could see a vein pulsing in Jon's neck as he continued. "I put up with you vetoing every choice I made. I let it go. I didn't say much when all you talked about morning, noon, and night was this house. You seem to forget how I dropped everything and picked up the kids from school on multiple occasions because you couldn't draw yourself away from another important meeting about flooring, backsplash tiles, tub styles...which wasn't easy for me, by the way!"

Jon was shouting now. Katie took several steps back as he

dumped his frustrations at her feet. An outburst of this magnitude was totally out of character for her husband. She couldn't remember the last time he'd raised his voice at her. Never had she seen him this angry.

The situation confused her, rattled her equilibrium. She always had a response, a good comeback in any difficult discussion. Not this time. This time she didn't quite know what to say. Especially since Jon was being totally off base.

"Oh, that's commendable, Jon. Should we make lists and compare? Who stood in the shadows while you were immersed in getting the restaurant up and running? Who helped prepare all the marketing materials and social media campaign? Who kept the household running while you were never home?"

Even as these things left her mouth, she cringed inside. She hated this...all of it.

Jon slumped onto the sofa, rubbed his forehead. "The big question remains. We had a budget. We're way over. How are we going to pay for it?"

"Yes, we're over budget," she admitted. "My father left us each money when he passed. I will use mine to cover the gap."

"Your inheritance money?" Jon cocked his head in disbelief. He stood and made his way into the kitchen and looked out the tiny window above the sink.

Neither of them said anything for several seconds. Finally, he broke his silence. "We agreed that would fund the girls' college expenses."

Katie opened the refrigerator and brought out a can of cola, popped the top, and took a long drink, trying to collect her thoughts. "We *talked* about it," Katie admitted, after giving his statement some thought. "I'm not certain a decision was made. We still have years to save for school."

Jon refused to back down. "Willa is likely to go to school on the mainland. Out-of-state tuition is going to drain our current account, let alone the extra travel expenses. Those expenses are only a few years away. Then we have Noelle."

Leaning her hip against the kitchen counter, Katie tried another approach. "I understand what you're saying, but we both make good money. Without that money we'd have had to rely on savings alone."

"But we did have that money," Jon argued. "And you sunk it in upgraded bathroom fixtures."

"You're being completely unfair!" She didn't mean to shout, to be so shrill, but her frustration level was rising. She could barely keep her growing anger in check. Did he think she was stupid? That she didn't know how to manage money?

Jon dropped his head and pressed his hands against his skull, like the escalation of their argument had grown too much for him to handle. When he finally looked up at her, he simply shook his head. "Fine. No amount of arguing is going to change anything. It's already done. The money is spent. You got your way. As always."

With that he turned and headed out the door, slamming it behind him.

Katie stood there, stunned. What had just happened?

She swallowed hard at his words and collapsed into a chair. She never meant to spend that much. Each expenditure seemed so reasonable at the time. One by one, they'd added up. Frankly, she was surprised to see the total.

Still, she'd carefully considered each decision and had optioned for the upgrades. There was little reason to cut corners when building the house of her dreams. Perhaps Jon had been right about her vetoing his choices, but clearly her husband had no decorating taste.

She was right to carefully maneuver the final outcome. Jasmit had agreed and complimented her on each decision. Never had she felt so respected, so listened to. Her opinions mattered. Her choices were commended. No longer was she simply in the shadows, ordering merchandise and putting it on the shelf day in and day out. Even Willa could do that.

Christel had multiple degrees. She was a CPA and an attorney. The success of Pali Maui depended on her knowledge and guidance.

Aiden ran an entire rescue station. He was the top dog.

No one would argue her mother was a force to be reckoned with. Her father passed and his absence barely caused a ripple in the operation. Everyone knew her mother was the one in charge, the one who had inherited Pali Maui and grew it into one of the largest and most respected business enterprises in all of Hawaii. Shipping magnates, financiers, CEOs of chain-branded hotels...they all admired her and deferred to her decisions and recommendations.

Even her Aunt Vanessa was a big deal...or at least she had been when she was a well-known news anchor in a big market. Then she got fired. But that was beside the point.

Katie's throat grew thick with emotion realizing she had accomplished very little. She had done nothing that her girls would admire when they grew up. She was ordinary.

Her fingertips brushed the runaway tear on her cheek. For once, while working on the house, she was doing what she was really good at. She was special. Capable. And necessary.

A banging at the door drew her attention. Katie barely had time to lift from the chair when the door flew open.

"Why aren't you and Jon answering your phones?" she demanded. "Willa is at school. She's in trouble."

13

"Get in the car. I'll drive you," Vanessa said as Katie grabbed her phone from the counter. She'd put it on silent and had neglected to switch it back when she and Jon got tangled in their argument.

They raced to the high school where they found Willa in the principal's office, sitting in a chair with her head pointed at the floor.

"Willa?" Katie asked. "What's going on?"

Her daughter looked up at her miserably.

Katie gasped. "Willa! What happened?"

Vanessa stood at the principal's office door, holding it open with her backside. "Looks like she plowed into a quarterback without her helmet on."

Tears sprouted in her daughter's eyes, one of which was turning shades of purple. Her hair was messed up and her lip swollen and bloodied.

Katie knelt and took her baby's hands in her own. "Oh, honey."

Paula Liebert rose from behind her desk. "I'm afraid there was an altercation."

Katie didn't bother to hide her shock. "An altercation? Willa was in a fight?" She glanced at her daughter for confirmation. "Who with?"

Willa folded her arms tightly against her chest. "Amanda Cooper and her gang."

Katie's hand flew to her chest. "There was more than one?" Her eyes narrowed. "Isn't Amanda Cooper the one who—"

Willa nodded. "Yup. That's the one."

"I thought you were friends," Katie insisted. Even as she said it, she recalled what her mother had told her earlier, how Amanda was being mean to Willa's new friend. She'd intended to take care of the matter, approach Amanda's mother and let her in on how her daughter had been acting toward Kina. Unfortunately, when Noelle came down with that rash, Katie had gotten distracted. Then, she simply forgot to follow up.

"The key word being *were*," Willa told her. "She's anything but a friend."

Katie had never thought the girl had proper supervision. Her parents seemed to be too tied up with their own lives to monitor their daughter's activities, including overseeing her dating. When she'd ended up the one who was pregnant, and not Willa, all those months back...well, she didn't fashion herself as judgmental, but clearly Amanda's parents fell short in their role.

Of course, this was not her shining moment, either. Her mom had alerted her there had been some bullying at school. Katie kicked herself for getting distracted and not dealing with the situation when she learned of it. She should have brought this to the school's attention right then, before things escalated.

Mrs. Liebert came around to the front of her desk and leaned on the front corner. "It appears a situation developed."

Before she could finish, Willa popped in with the full story. "Amanda Cooper is a bully!" She turned to her mother, wincing as she moved. "She's been hassling Kina for weeks, just because she can. The final straw was this morning when she made fun of Kina's shoes. Asked her if she'd pulled them from the dumpster, saying most of what Kina wore was discards no one else wanted."

Katie's hand went to her mouth in shock. "Oh, she didn't!"

Willa nodded. "Yes, she did. I'd had enough. I plowed into her. One thing led to another and—"

Her Aunt Vanessa didn't wait for her to finish. "And soon all of Amanda's friends piled into the argument. Am I right?"

"Yeah," Willa confirmed. "I wasn't the first to swing, but I swung the hardest." She lifted her chin. "I'd do it again."

Vanessa thrust an index finger toward her. "That's right, you would."

Katie bit down hard. "Not helpful, Aunt Vanessa," she murmured, refraining from kicking at her aunt's feet.

Mrs. Liebert steepled her fingers on her desk. "There will be a full investigation of the matter, and I promise all proper recourse will be taken." She looked over at Katie. "Unfortunately, school policy requires that I suspend Willa for three days."

"Three days?" Katie asked, incredulous that her daughter was being punished for defending a friend against a bully. "What about Amanda?"

"Same," Mrs. Liebert advised. "While I agree, this situation is extremely disturbing—this school will not tolerate bullying of any sort—it is important that all the girls involved learn that disagreements are not resolved with physical force."

Willa shrugged. "It was worth it."

Vanessa casually asked, "What about Kina? Where is she in all of this?"

"Her mother was called and she's also waiting to be picked up. As far as we can ascertain, Kina was not involved in the physical fight. If we're able to confirm that, she won't be subject to suspension."

Willa shook her head. "She wasn't involved, except to be the brunt of Amanda's taunts. She's a real b—"

"Willa!" Katie scolded before her daughter could finish her sentence.

"Beyoncé, Mom. I was going to say Amanda is a real Beyoncé."

Vanessa frowned. "Want to interpret for us old people?"

"Amanda considers herself a celebrity and thinks she can shake it for anybody, ignore everybody and smack anybody down at whim."

"Sounds like a real gem," Vanessa muttered under her breath.

14

"Where are you taking us?" Aimee glanced over her shoulder at Carson, who was fastened safely in his car seat in the back.

"I have a surprise," Shane explained, beaming. "A big surprise."

She checked her reflection in the sun visor mirror. "I'd have thought you'd run out of surprises after that stunt at the beach." She lifted her hand, appreciating the glint in her engagement ring. "This ring really is beautiful," she sighed.

She leaned and brushed a kiss against Shane's cheek, immediately bringing a smile to his face. Shane was genuinely happy, and from the look on Aimee's face, she felt the same. Never before had he felt so settled. Instead of drifting from day to day, focusing on a good time, he looked to the future. A real future, with Aimee and Carson.

"Okay, close your eyes," he instructed as he pulled up to the gate at the entrance to the neighborhood. Wimberly Ann was standing by her car on the other side. She pushed the remote box and motioned him in.

"Okay, open!" he told Aimee, barely able to hold in his excitement.

Aimee slowly opened her eyes. She frowned. "I don't understand. Where are we?"

Wimberly Ann waved her manicured hand in their direction.

Aimee pointed. "And who is that?"

"Ta-da! That's our realtor," Shane explained. "She's going to show us some houses."

This made Aimee even more confused. "Houses?"

Shane nodded eagerly. "We can't easily raise a family in that tiny shanty, can we?" He put the car in gear and followed Wimberly Ann's vehicle until she came to a stop in front of the house they'd looked at the other day. Of the three, this one was his favorite. Even so, he'd let Aimee choose which they would put earnest money down on.

"Can we afford this?" she asked. "I mean, I just got my old job back. Tips are good, but not mortgage good."

Shane explained about the money he'd inherited while he was unfastening Carson from the car seat. "We can't get crazy. I mean, we still have a budget. Wimberly Ann is going to show us a few today. You can choose which one we'll buy."

Aimee beamed. "Are you kidding? Wow!"

Wimberly Ann approached. Today she was wearing a tight-fitted sleeveless dress in yellow. She'd clipped her hair back with an ornamental fake plumeria of the same color. "Well, hey, you two. Are you ready to purchase a house?" she asked.

Shane made introductions. Wimberly Ann cooed over Carson, who had just woken up. The baby's face brightened into a wide smile, leaving deep dimples in his cheeks.

"Aren't you just darling?" Wimberly pinched his cheek lightly before turning to them. "Well, let's take a look at this house."

The front of the two-story structure was painted blue with

white trim. Aimee clapped her hands together. "Blue is my favorite color," she exclaimed. Shane thought this was a good sign.

His fiancée also loved the spacious living space, the kitchen cabinetry, and the master bedroom with the ensuite bath.

"The location is top notch," Wimberly Ann explained. She removed a copy of the listing from her clipboard and handed it to Aimee. "The schools are highly desirable and you have grocery stores nearby." She winked. "And a Starbucks."

That seemed to sell Aimee. "I love it. I want this one."

"Are you sure?" Shane asked, hoping she wouldn't change her mind.

"Oh, yes. Did you see the bedroom with the big window overlooking the palm trees in the backyard? That would make the perfect nursery. And later, when Carson is older, we'll move him upstairs and convert the nursery into the guest room. Or an office."

Wimberly Ann was quick to jump on the notion that a sale was imminent. "Excellent! I'll get the paperwork together and bring it over to you this evening to sign." She turned to Shane. "You'll need to have a cashier's check ready for the earnest money," she told him.

"No problem. I can go to the bank this afternoon." Shane's heart pounded a bit faster. It was one thing to consider buying a home. It was another when the idea became reality. "We'll see you tonight."

He reached his arm around Aimee's shoulder and pulled her against him. "Looks like we're going to be homeowners."

15

"What do you mean, Willa got in a fight at school?" Jon stopped running water over a colander filled with leeks and set it on the stainless-steel counter next to the sink. "Why didn't you call me? I'd have gone with you." Katie knew from the tone he used that he was frustrated with her, again.

Katie wondered herself why she hadn't called Jon before jetting to the school with Aunt Vanessa. Even though she didn't know all the details, she knew something was up with their daughter. Honestly, her argument with Jon was still fresh and raw and she simply hadn't wanted to deal with him.

The thought was unsettling. "I don't know," she lied. "I should have. I was upset and Aunt Vanessa offered to drive me. So, I went. Besides, you were already going to be late for work thanks to our little discussion," she said, not hiding the fact she was still miffed. "I figured I could handle whatever it was."

She explained to Jon what had happened, how Amanda Cooper had treated Willa's new friend and how the behavior had been going on for a while now. "She's the worst kind of bully," she told Jon.

Her husband ran a hand through his hair. "Well, I'm opposed to our daughter physically fighting. There are better ways of reacting. Coming to us, for one. I have to admit, I am a little proud of her for sticking up for Kina."

"Me, too," Katie admitted. "So, we're in agreement. No punishment?"

"Sounds like the school handled that. A suspension is a bit harsh, given the circumstances, but they have their rules." Jon turned away from her. "I'll be late tonight."

Without saying anything more, he exited the kitchen and headed for the cooler. Not so much as a hug, a kiss, or even a thank-you for handling the situation.

He's still mad and that's fine, she thought. She was mad, too.

Yet this coldness between them was completely foreign to her. Sure, they had occasional skiffs. Any minor disagreement was quickly resolved through compromise…often Jon giving in to her.

She headed home, trying to tell herself he had blown this budget thing all out of proportion. Yet inside, she knew he had a point. She had gone over budget.

He simply didn't understand how important this house build was to her. Hadn't she fully supported him when he quit a good-paying job to risk starting the restaurant. Hadn't the business endeavor initially cleaned out their savings?

She'd believed in him. When he'd questioned whether he'd done the right thing, she buoyed him up and assured him the restaurant would be a big hit once word spread. She was right. No Ke 'Oi became one of the most sought-after dining venues on the island. Not only did Jon make a tidy sum, but the restaurant drew tourists to Pali Maui—a win for her entire family.

While this house she'd worked so hard to build may not be a profit-making venture, it was all in your perspective. Didn't she have the right to feel as much pride in her endeavor?

Of course, she did. Jon was simply being unfair.

Her husband returned, wiping his hands on a kitchen towel. He was followed by his sous chef.

Jon seemed surprised to see her still there. "Where is Willa now?" he asked.

"She's in her room, studying," she told him.

"Fine. I'll talk with her when I get home." He turned for the sink.

Katie waited for the sous chef to step out of hearing distance. Maybe it was time to remind her husband how much work she did for him. "I need the verbiage for the changes you want on the website."

"I gave that to you yesterday." He flipped the towel over his shoulder.

"No, you didn't."

Jon fished the phone from his pocket and clicked a few times, then shoved the screen in front of her face.

She blinked rapidly. "Well, I didn't see it."

"Well, maybe you were distracted...with the house stuff," he countered.

Her blood boiled. Before she could form an appropriate retort, he lifted the colander from the counter. "Like I said, I'll talk to Willa when I get home." He turned to the sink and flipped the water back on.

"Fine," she said to his back. Hurt and angry, she turned and stomped out.

She was halfway back to the shanty when a car approached and pulled to a stop. Out climbed a woman. She immediately reminded her of a blonde bombshell who just stepped off a vintage Hollywood screen.

"Hey, honey! I'm here to meet with Shane Briscoe and his fiancé. Could you direct me to where he lives?" She pointed to the row of shanties.

Before Katie could respond, a man's voice from behind her answered. "Second one from the end, ma'am." She turned to find Mig.

"Oh, thank you," the woman cooed, clearly impressed with their farm manager. She reached to straighten her short, tight-fitted blue skirt. In the process, some of the papers from the stack she held in her hand fluttered to the ground. She bent to retrieve them.

Mig quickly stepped forward. "Here, let me."

"That's so nice of you." The woman wore a white blouse made of slinky material cut low to reveal her ample cleavage. Her pumps were high, so high she wobbled slightly as she moved back to allow Mig's help.

He handed her the dropped papers. Her face broke into a wide smile and a business card appeared in her manicured hand. "I'm Wimberly Ann Jenkins. And you are?"

Mig's face reddened slightly. "Miguel Nakamoa. Friends call me Mig."

"Well," she purred. "I know we've just met, but I hope to count myself in that group...Mig."

Flustered, he buried his attention on the card. "You're a realtor."

"Yes, I am! I'm helping Shane and Aimee buy a house."

Katie's eyes flew open wide. "Shane's buying a house?" This was news. She wondered if the rest of her family knew about this. "When did all this come about?"

"He reached out to me a few days ago," Wimberly Ann reported. "Those two are such a cute couple, and delightful to work with."

"I don't think Shane and Aimee are home right now," Katie told her, still trying to digest what she'd just learned. "I saw them leave in the car about an hour ago. I'm sure if you had an appointment, they'll be back any time."

The realtor's gaze remained on Mig. "No problem. I'm happy to wait."

Mig shifted on his feet. "Well, I need to get back to work. It was nice meeting you, Ms. Jenkins."

"My friends call me Wimberly Ann," she said, winking. She tapped the hand that held the card. "I hope you'll give me a call sometime. That's my cell. Reach out anytime you have need of a realtor." She paused before adding, "Or a friend." She smiled at Mig suggestively.

Mig didn't seem to know how to respond to her bold invitation. He thanked her and tucked her card in his shirt pocket before he headed in the direction of the packing sheds, glancing back over his shoulder...twice.

"Oh, isn't he daaar...ling." Her hand went to her chest. "A real man's man. Some women prefer suits, but I'm a flannel girl all the way."

"A flannel?" Katie asked, puzzled.

"Yes, I prefer a man who wears jeans and work shirts. Especially if they look like him." She pointed her thumb in his direction. "I didn't see a ring on Mig's finger, so I assume he's single?"

Katie confirmed that he was. Had been for years.

None of them thought he'd ever remarry. Despite plenty of opportunities, Mig had never dated since his wife left him. Rumor had it, his ex-wife had a terrible temper. Katie's mom could hear her screaming at him at night when the windows were open.

Mig never responded in kind. She was told he continued to love her and provide for her and their young daughter, even when his wife failed to come home at night. Despite the woman's poor treatment, he was lost when she left him.

Thankfully, he and his daughter continued to bond over the summers when he had custody. Leilani now lived in Honolulu and worked in book publicity. They were still close.

And when Katie's mother learned of her father's infidelity, it was Mig who offered silent support. When someone splits your life in two and you're sinking in the aftermath, someone who's been there can provide a lifeline.

Thankfully, Shane and Aimee pulled up moments later, relieving Katie of the need to entertain his realtor.

"Sorry," Shane said. "We had to stop for diapers."

"It was my fault," Aimee claimed, taking all the blame. "I let us run low."

Wimberly Ann turned to Katie. "Aren't they just the cutest?"

The minute they proceeded inside Shane's place, Katie grabbed her phone and dialed Aiden. "Did you know Shane is buying a house?" she asked the minute he picked up.

"What? A house. Shane?"

"Yes, he's meeting with the realtor now. Apparently, he contacted her days ago and they are now signing papers of some sort."

"What kind of papers?" Aiden prompted.

"I don't know. But it's clear they are far down the line on this thing. Our little brother is buying a house. I think he's putting earnest money down."

"Does he even know what earnest money is?" Katie knew what he was saying and felt the same thing. Aiden's voice confirmed her own reservations. Shane had jumped out and done this on his own with little help or advice from his family. Even more disconcerting was how he was acting like no one the family even knew. He'd dropped his carefree lifestyle and had suddenly become Mr. Responsible. Was this an act, or was their younger brother being authentic?

"It matters little now what he knows about earnest money, or mortgage rates, or amortization schedules, for that matter." Exhaling slowly, Katie told him about Wimberly Ann Jenkins. "She's a shark, Aiden. Something's off here. I mean, she's nice and all...but I'm not sure she's giving him the full picture. I see dollar signs behind those fake lashes."

"Eh, don't be too quick to judge," her brother warned.

"Just wait until you see her." Katie paused for emphasis. "Then tell me not to judge." She went on to reel off the interaction between Wimberly Ann and Mig. She told him about the lowcut blouse and how bold she became when their farm manager showed up on the scene.

Surprisingly, this made Aiden break out in laughter. "Mig's a big boy. He's fully capable of handling pushy women. He'll keep a level head."

"I don't know," Katie countered. "You didn't see the look in his eyes."

16

Ava pressed the final shrimp onto the skewer next to a chunk of pineapple. Moving day had finally arrived and Jon and Katie were spending the first night in their newly built home. To celebrate, the family was gathering at their place.

Ava was serving all the family's favorite pineapple recipes. She'd cooked all day—pineapple chicken skewers, pineapple coconut rice, salmon filets glazed with jalapeño pineapple jam. For dessert, her delicious pineapple rum cake and a bucket of frozen Dole Whip for the children.

Plugging in her earbuds, she set about finishing up her kitchen duties and texted Willa and Shane to come help her take everything to the party.

Jon and Katie's house had, indeed, turned out lovely—a stunning display of open-air grandeur and ocean vistas. She especially envied the natural construction materials and the three-hundred-sixty-degree wrap-around deck.

Granted, the build had surpassed everyone's expectations. Even so, she worried her ambitious daughter had overextended their finances, amounts they wouldn't get back. Especially since they'd agreed to the stipulation she'd placed on the gifted lot—that the lot would never be subdivided and they'd never sell.

One of the hardest parts of being a parent to adult children was backing off and allowing them to make their decisions without input and advice. She was as capable as anyone of pushing her ideas onto her children. She loved them and only wanted the best. Long ago, Lincoln had taken her aside and redirected her intentions. "They must learn on their own, just as we did," he reminded.

She wondered what he would think of everything that had transpired since he left them. The Briscoe family had experienced so much since that day.

She'd discovered his infidelity and cruel choice of partners —the daughter of her best friend. Despite his betrayal, she had survived...even thrived, thanks to a loving family and close friends. Alani and Elta had walked through the hurt as well. Together, they lifted each other as they learned there was a path to forgiveness. Her brother, Jack, had helped her embrace a life of joy. "It's the best way to get even," he'd told her. "Be happy."

Aiden had been in a horrible accident, one that frightened them terribly. Thankfully, he didn't suffer any lifelong injuries, in part because his recovery was at the hands of a highly respected surgeon who seemed to have captured her daughter Christel's heart. Katie and Jon continued to raise their two darling girls. Their house fire was the impetus for building a new home at Pali Maui. Now, they lived closer to her, a fact that made her even happier.

Shane was surprised when his former girlfriend, now fiancé, showed up with a surprise baby...an adorable little boy named Carson. That baby had captured all of their hearts, most especially her son's. He and Aimee would be married soon in a small ceremony at Wailea Chapel, with Elta officiating. She imagined it would be beautiful. Despite predictions to the contrary, Shane had grown up.

Now, she'd learned her son was in the process of buying a home. Lincoln always suggested she spoiled Shane, that he would never learn to be responsible if she kept coddling him. Lincoln had been wrong...about that and many other things.

Even in Lincoln's absence, Pali Maui was flourishing. She and Christel, with Katie and Mig's help, had increased production by twenty percent and had entered into shipping contracts that allowed overseas delivery in four additional countries. Under Katie's guidance, they'd expanded the gift store and tour operation. Jon's restaurant's reputation grew, and so did Pali Maui's profit margins. Soon, they would be expanding the onsite golf course to include manicured greens and fairways that would rival any first-rate country club.

Thirty minutes later, Willa and Shane showed up. Together, they carted the food items into the car, drove the short distance to Jon and Katie's new home, and went about the task of unloading.

"Can I help you?" Aimee asked as she approached the car.

"Why, thank you. Yes. Grab that bucket of Dole Whip." Ava pointed. "It needs to go in the freezer right away."

Mig arrived to the party soon after, followed by Christel and Evan. Christel was no longer using crutches but still had a noticeable limp.

The entire family gathered, along with Elta and Alani and their son, Ori. Kina and her mother, Halia, were also there, as were Ava's brother, Jack, and her sister, Vanessa.

Alani tilted her head back and gazed at the soaring ceilings with wooden beam rafters. "I've never seen anything this stunning," she murmured, praising Katie's choices.

Katie beamed. "Thank you. It turned out even better than we'd hoped."

While the others were dishing up their plates, Katie glanced around the room for Jon, who was nowhere to be seen. "Have you seen my husband?" she asked Aiden.

"Not since when I first got here," he told her.

Katie wandered the house, peeking in rooms to see where her husband had escaped to. Finally, she spotted him standing out on the deck, alone.

She excused herself and moved to join him. "Jon? What are you doing out here?" she asked.

"I needed some air," was his quick retort.

"Well, come inside," she urged. "We're hosting a party."

Jon huffed. "I'm not in a celebratory mood."

Her eyes widened with surprise. "You're not still mad? Are you?"

"Not mad. I don't particularly care to join in on the oohing and aahing." He said this as if he had a bad taste in his mouth. "Especially given our empty bank account."

She quickly motioned for him to lower his voice so the others didn't hear their little spat. "Look, we can take this up later. Right now, family and friends are all inside. It's rude for you to remain out here." She folded her arms and waited.

"Well, we wouldn't want that." His words dripped with sarcasm.

"Look, I'm sorry. Okay? I should have talked to you before approving the overages." Even as she said this, she knew her instincts had told her it would be better to move ahead and ask forgiveness later. Admittedly, she'd do it again if time reversed and she faced the decision all over. She'd never confess that to Jon.

Katie drew a deep breath. "Honey, I know you worry. I love how you take care of our finances. But, Jon...goodness, you make it sound like it was the worst thing in the world. I regret not including you in these decisions, but can't we just move past this? There's little that can be done now to change anything." In an attempt to smooth things over, she reached and stroked the side of his face.

In a surprise move, Jon brushed her hand away. "I got you—you have regrets, yet every time you open your mouth, your logic makes everything worse. Let's go with you're sorry and leave it at that."

Her mouth gaped open. Stunned at his rebuff, she reluctantly agreed. "Fine. We won't ever discuss it again. Right now, we have guests inside and we're being rude. Can you put your pout aside for a couple of hours?" Without waiting for a reply, she turned and headed for the party.

"Sure, let's go celebrate," he murmured and reluctantly followed her into their new home.

Ava sat on the arm chair with her hand resting on Willa's shoulder. "There you are," she said. She glanced between Katie and Jon. Something was up between the two of them. Jon was acting abnormally reserved. Typically, her son-in-law was jovial and right in the middle of things. He often could be seen winking at his wife and holding her hand.

Katie looked like she'd bitten into a sour pickle.

Things between them were definitely chilly.

She suspected the friction had to do with the house. Her daughter could be obstinate and self-focused. Jon was laid back and easygoing. He gave into her more times than not. Clearly, her daughter had expensive taste and had gone high-end throughout the build. It didn't take a genius to surmise Jon wasn't fond of Jasmit Tan, while Katie fawned all over the famous architect and took each of his design recommendations to heart.

Katie took after her father. Lincoln made decisions out of emotion. Ava carefully calculated consequences. This caused them to rub each other wrong often.

Her heart squeezed a little. Had that tension contributed to Lincoln's affair?

Suddenly, Willa let out a shriek. She clutched her phone, her hands trembling.

Alarmed, Ava quickly asked what was wrong. "Honey, what it is?"

Her granddaughter's eyes immediately filled with tears. Her chin quivered. "Amanda Cooper just sent out a picture over all her social media accounts."

Both Katie and Jon rushed over. "What kind of picture?"

Willa thrust the phone into her mother's hands.

Katie gasped. "What is this?" she asked, horrified.

Jon took the phone. His face darkened. "Where did this come from?"

Willa choked back a sob. "It's not real. It's photoshopped."

Dread filled Ava as she lifted from the chair and looked over Jon's shoulder. There on the phone was a photo of Willa, topless and seductively posing.

Her hand flew to her chest. "Oh, my! How did she—"

Everyone within earshot quickly gathered to check out the commotion. Kina needled her way to the center of the circle. Upon seeing the photo, she almost growled. "That Amanda Cooper is evil!"

Willa grabbed her phone from her dad's hand and shut it off. "Everyone is going to believe that is me!" she cried. "I don't want *anyone* to see that photo."

Even as the words escaped Willa's mouth—Ava, along with everyone standing in that room, knew Willa's wishes were mute.

Phones were likely pinging even as they all stood there. Lots of people, including Willa's teachers and fellow students, would see that photo.

17

Willa ran from the room and scrambled up the floating staircase to her room. Her door slammed. Kina hurried up after her.

Katie felt her knees go weak. "Jon, do something!"

"You bet I'll do something," he assured her. Anger darkened his face. "I'm heading over to the Coopers right now. Heads are going to roll."

"Wait!" Aiden cautioned, in the commotion that followed. "That might not be such a great idea. In my line of work, I see these kinds of incidents often. Direct confrontation can lead to ugly places. The best thing to do is call law enforcement. Let them deal with this."

"Yes," Elta said. "Let's everyone take a minute and calm down."

Ori moaned. He held up his own phone. "There's a second photograph. This one is of Kina."

"What?" Halia hesitated, as if afraid to confirm what he said was true. Finally, she reached for his phone and took a look for herself. "Oh, no!" she cried, her voice choked with emotion. She reluctantly handed the phone back before directing her attention back to Jon and Katie. "This is awful. What kind of person would do such a thing?" She shook her head in disbelief. "What do we do? How do we get these down?"

Shane handed off Carson into Aimee's arms. "Well, I know this. Once something is on social media, there's really no way to truly remove it. I mean an image can be deleted, but that doesn't keep others from saving the image...or from posting and sharing. These things can take on a life of their own."

Alani threw up her dimpled hands in frustration. "Ay, what is the world coming to?"

"Well, I'm going to see to it those images are down!" Jon stormed. "No matter what it takes."

Katie turned her attention to the second floor, to Willa's closed bedroom door. "I need to go talk with her," she said, moving in the direction of the stairs. Shane caught her arm. "Let me, Sis."

She hesitated. She knew her girl. Willa needed her mother right now. Yet something inside whispered her little brother might be just the one who could give her comfort. He was closer in age and certainly more experienced about cyberbullying. He may even be able to pose a solution of some kind." She growled inside. "It was unthinkable that a young girl would stoop so low. And to think Amanda Cooper had spent time in her home, eaten at her dinner table. What had happened to the girl she once thought she knew?

"Your brother's right," Jon agreed. He turned to his wife. "Let Shane go." He looked at her, this time his eyes filled with kindness. When it came to the wellbeing of their daughters, all conflict was moved aside.

Katie didn't argue. Instead, she reached for Jon's hand.

"In addition to the police, perhaps the school authorities should be notified," Ava suggested. "I mean, I'm no expert here, but it seems to me this situation will carry down the school hallways come Monday morning."

"That's a good idea," Evan said. His arm went around Christel's waist and he gave a supportive hug.

Christal voiced her agreement. "There may be other incidents," she suggested. "Even if there are no prior issues, the school officials will want to know. And, yes. You should absolutely report this to the police," she added.

Jon agreed and pulled his phone from his pocket and dialed. When they answered, he stepped aside to make the report.

"Why is Katie's friend doing this?" Aiden asked.

Katie quickly corrected him. "Ex-friend." She explained the earlier incident at the school and how Willa had a physical altercation with Amanda Cooper and her compadre of fellow bullies. Willa had stood up for Kina when horribly unkind things were said. She was proud of her daughter. She certainly didn't deserve this. Even if she did get physical.

"Oh, honey," Ava said. "Why didn't you tell me?"

Katie shrugged. "Willa didn't want anyone to know. You all know how out of character that is for Willa to plow into some gal." She directed her attention to Halia. "Like I said, she was protecting Kina. Amanda was saying mean and hurtful things. Willa simply wouldn't tolerate someone being hurtful."

Halia nodded. "Yes, where that Cooper girl goes, trouble seems to follow." She paused. "But this? Posting explicit photos—real or not—well, that's completely unacceptable."

"Intolerable," Katie added. She didn't need to look to her husband for confirmation that he was with her on this. Still, she sought his eyes out. "And we not going to let this pass, are we, Jon?"

He wholeheartedly said he would not let this go. He grabbed Katie's hand. "You all can continue eating. Katie and I are going to nip this in the bud. This stops right now."

Halia offered to go with them. "If you think it'd be of any help. I want to be supportive." The look on her face said the opposite. Kina's mother was likely prone to solving most problems with essential oils and meditation. This was out of her comfort zone.

"No, you stay. I think it's best if Katie and I confront this one," Jon told her.

Less than a half an hour later, they pulled up in front of Amanda Cooper's house. Jon shut off the engine. Katie reached for his hand. "You're shaking."

"I'm so mad, I could kill that kid."

"Jon, me too. But we need to be careful here." She wasn't used to seeing her husband this angry. Guilt weighed on her.

"It's my fault," Katie admitted, quietly, with her hand on the door handle. "There were red flags. I knew of the bullying. I let distractions keep me from addressing it earlier."

Jon nodded. "No one could have anticipated this," he said, relieving her of some of her guilt. "We both let our daughter down when we believed this bullying would resolve on its own."

They got out of the car and moved in unison to the Coopers' front door. Katie lifted her hand and pushed the doorbell.

They waited. Nothing.

She pressed the doorbell a second time.

They waited. Still no answer.

"Looks like nobody is home," Katie murmured.

They were turning to leave when the door cracked open. Before they could open their mouths to speak, the door slammed shut.

Jon's jaw set. He pounded on the door. "If that's you, Amanda, I have something I need to say."

A car engine pulled their attention to the curb. Amanda's mother killed the motor and got out. She wore a tight pair of jeans, an off-the-shoulder jersey top, and a frown. "Can I help you?" she called out.

Recognition dawned on the woman's face as she moved toward them. "You're Katie's mom."

"Yes," Katie confirmed. This was the second time they'd met face-to-face. "We're here because we have a problem."

"If you're talking about the fight at school, there's nothing more to say. The school officials dealt with it. The end."

She proceeded to circle around them. Jon stepped in her path, blocking her. "I suggest you hear us out," he said, his voice more menacing than Katie knew he intended.

His tone also seemed to surprise Amanda's mother. "Fine. What do you want?" She glanced between them. "But make it short. I have an important date tonight, and I'm running late."

Willa was right. This woman wouldn't win any Mother of the Year awards. She appeared completely nonplussed by two parents showing up at her door wanting to discuss an important issue with her daughter.

Katie clenched her fists at her side. If that woman smacked her gum one more time, she swore she would reach inside her mouth and pull it out.

Thankfully, Jon seemed to have better control. "Let me be direct. Amanda just posted a salacious photo of our daughter and another of her friend, Kina, both on social media. The photos are extremely explicit and—"

"And they're not even *real*," Katie pointed out, interrupting. "They are digitally altered."

Amanda's mother shrugged. "Are you sure?"

"Am I sure of what?" Katie demanded.

The woman slowly raised her eyebrows and stared. "Are you sure the photographs aren't real? And how do you know it was Amanda who posted the photos? There are over a thousand students in that high school. Any one of them could have done it."

Katie could see Jon was struggling to maintain his temper. "I guess it's time I take another tack—I will be making a written police report. Cyberbullying is against the law. There are plenty of means for tracking ISP addresses. Law enforcement will be able to trace the post to your daughter's phone in no time. Did you know that distributing child pornography carries a very hefty penalty? His voice was low, calculating, solid. "Your daughter is out of control. She went too far. And now my daughter will have to live with the fallout. But as we speak, the officers from the Maui Police Department are headed to our house. We will give a full account of everything that has transpired between the girls—and especially this last stunt. Your daughter has committed a felony." He huffed. "Let the bricks fall where they may."

At this, Amanda's mother's earlier confidence crumbled. "Child pornography, that's a malicious accusation. Besides, she a minor. She'll only get a slap on the wrist."

"Are you sure of that?"

Amanda's mother swallowed and took a step back. He'd broken her armor. Good.

The front door suddenly swung open and Amanda appeared on the doorstep. "Go right ahead and report it," she challenged. "There were two similar incidents last year. Both were reported to the police and nothing happened to those kids." She laughed. "To be honest, nothing will happen to me either. There are much bigger fish. They get a half-dozen reports every day of kids stealing stuff out of tourists' rental cars."

"Shut up, Amanda." Her mom pointed a finger in the girl's direction. Her hands were trembling.

Jon pulled a folded card from his shirt pocket. "Do you know what this is, Amanda?"

She rolled her eyes.

"This is a scorecard from the golf course at Pali Maui. I'm showing it to you because just last week I played golf with the police chief, who is a close friend of my brother-in-law, who, by the way, is the top dog at Maui Rescue. They're real tight, the chief and him."

Jon took a step closer to the girl. "My first call was to him. He promised to handle this situation personally. There will be big trouble to follow unless you get those photos down. And. I. Mean. Down. Now!" He leaned forward. "Otherwise, you may as well pack a bag, because you're going to spend the night in jail."

Amanda paled. She threw a helpless look to her mother. "But, I—"

Jon took another step. "NOW, AMANDA. Get those pictures down now."

She nodded, eyes wide, and ran inside.

Jon looked at Amanda's mother. If Katie knew her husband, he was struggling with reeling in his anger toward the woman standing before him.

"I'm sorry," Amanda's mother mumbled. "It has been hard since her dad left."

Jon worked the muscle in his jaw.

She rubbed her collarbone. "I think you're aware Amanda got pregnant. She hasn't been okay since."

Jon let out a long breath. "But she doesn't have the right to ruin another girl's life. Not ever. Get her some counseling. Or your troubles are just beginning."

Katie stared up at her husband wondering who he was. Such wisdom, such strength in what was one of the most horrible situations they'd ever experienced.

Jon squared his shoulders and continued, "Teens need direction and adults who care enough to discipline them."

"Yeah, I get it," Amanda's mother said, lifting her chin defensively. "My daughter's the product of really bad parenting."

"You can turn this on yourself, if that makes you feel better. But what Amanda needs is professional help. You can step up and be there for her or not. That's on you. It's never too late to start being a good parent."

At that, Amanda opened the door and held out her phone. "Okay, the pics are down. I told my friends not to repost, that I was in deep crap. Enough?"

"Just curious. Are you even a little ashamed of yourself, Amanda?" Jon asked her.

Katie shot him a questioning look. Where was her husband going with this?

"Are you embarrassed?" Jon pressed. "At all?"

Amanda set her jaw, but her bottom lip quivered, betraying her. "Kinda."

"Good," Jon said, and gave a nod. "You need to remember this feeling so you'll never ever do anything like this again."

Jon and Katie exchanged glances. Jon turned back to Amanda and slowly rubbed at his cheek. Katie knew he wanted to continue, but he restrained himself. Instead, he simply said, "You can be better than this, Amanda."

With that, he grabbed Katie's hand and they turned and headed for their car.

After a nearly silent ride home, they arrived to find the house empty. The party had wrapped up without them. The kitchen had been cleaned and garbage taken out. Her mom left a note that she had the girls.

Katie was suddenly aware of how bone-tired she'd become. Conflict was not her thing, and she'd faced a lot of it today. First, Jon's expressed displeasure and then this situation with Amanda Cooper.

Gone was her enthusiasm for her first night in the new house. All eagerness to cook in her new kitchen, bathe in her new copper tub, and sleep in that master bedroom with the sliding doors open, the ocean breeze blowing gently across their new king bed—the wonder had evaporated. All of those things had dulled and mattered little right now.

Her family was the only thing that counted, and that Willa would be okay.

Jon made a call to the police chief and explained what had transpired at Amanda's house. The chief told him it wasn't too late to press charges and Jon said they could wait a day or two and see if the photos were, in fact, down.

Katie texted with her mom and asked if the girls were okay. Her mom reported they were fine and asked if the girls could stay over. Family had, no doubt, swooped in and comforted her, so Katie felt good about not disturbing the girls tonight since they were settled in. They'd all deal with the fallout of the photo tomorrow.

Katie turned to face Jon. "I'm tired and going to bed." She gave him a weak smile, mentally setting their earlier differences aside. There would be time for all that later, as well. "You were a rock star today," she told him. "Thank you for taking care of the situation."

The compliment brightened the look on his face. "We make a great team, especially when it comes to our kids."

Suddenly, her husband's hands went to the sides of her waist. He lifted her onto the kitchen island and gently pressed her down against the marble countertop.

"What are you doing?" she asked with utter surprise.

"Shh..." Jon placed his forefinger against her mouth. He unbuttoned her blouse. Then he leaned and kissed her chin, moving next to her neck. He continued, slowly moving down, kissing until he met resistance of her bra.

"I'm sorry I was a jerk earlier," he whispered against her skin. With one swift movement, his hand slipped under the back of her shirt and unfastened the hook.

Now breathless, she whispered against his chest. "Me too. I'm really sorry, Jon." And she meant it. She loved this house, but she loved her husband more. She'd been a fool to put him second.

Jon was fiercely protective, yet compassionate. He refrained from making decisions out of emotion, instead showing strength in his restraint. Not exactly something she was good at.

No matter what, even when they didn't see things the same way, she loved him and counted herself lucky to be his wife.

She showed him that now by returning his passion.

When they'd finished, Jon rolled over onto his back, staring up at the expensive lighting. His perspiring face broke into a wide grin. "I have to say...I really like the marble you chose for the countertop."

"You do?" she said, breathless. His inuendo did not go unnoticed. "It's imported. From Italy."

"Leave it to the Italians." He laughed out loud.

And Katie laughed with him.

18

Christel finished payroll and shut down her Mac. It was lunchtime and she was starved. Often, she'd bring leftovers from home and eat at her desk. At times, she'd choose to get away from her desk for a few minutes, so she'd go over to the restaurant and treat herself with one of Jon's entrees. If the scales in her bathroom weren't particularly against her that morning, she'd slip in a slice of sticky toffee banana cake.

Jon updated his menus daily, and Christel had access to the digital copy on the company's server, which came in extremely handy. She got first dibs on featured items that often sold out.

Before she could retrieve her purse from her desk drawer, the door to her office opened with Shane on the other side. "Hey, Sis. You busy?"

"I was just heading over to the restaurant to grab some lunch. Want to join me?"

That's when she noticed the sack in his hand. He held it up. "I brought us some hamburgers and fries," he announced, grinning.

"Wow, that's nice of you." She invited him to sit at her small conference table.

Christel didn't have the heart to tell him she rarely ate greasy fast food. Not only did it put on pounds but she felt a thousand percent better when she refrained from those types of meals. She highly suspected he ate nothing but.

Shane pointed at her ankle. "How's the sprain?"

"Mostly, fine. Now, it only hurts if I step down the wrong way." She dug into the small brown bag. "So, what's up. Why the visit?" She laid the hamburger and container of fries on a spread-out paper napkin. "I mean, this is a rarity."

"I need some advice," Shane admitted.

Christel granted him a smile. Knowledgeable older sister was a role she relished. "What kind of advice?"

"Well, Mom is pushing us to hold our wedding ceremony at Wailea Chapel."

Christel picked up her burger and pulled the paper back from the sandwich. "Not surprising. Go on."

"Well, it's like this. Aimee and I talked. She doesn't want a big fancy wedding. We really want something with just the family and only a few close friends. People like Mig and the Kanés."

"Why do you think that's a problem?" She took a bite of the hamburger, chewed while listening.

"There's more. We want to hold the ceremony at the Banana Patch." He watched for her reaction.

Christel dropped her burger to the napkin and quickly swallowed. "What in the world is the Banana Patch?"

He shoved a fry in his mouth and talked while he chewed. "You know Willa's new friend, Kina? Well, her mom is part owner of a retreat center spa thing called Banana Patch. They are just getting it off the ground. I think Halia and Kina struggle financially."

"Didn't there used to be a place by that name? A long time ago?"

Shane shrugged. "Before my time."

That made Christal laugh. "Most things are before your time, baby brother."

"So, what do you think?" He grabbed another fry. "Is Mom going to freak out?"

Christel pondered that a moment. Their mother never became pushy. Her nature was to be restrained when offering advice or guidance, always allowing room for her children and others to make their own decisions. Sure, she influenced...but her approach was subtle. "Mom will support whatever you two want; you know that. That doesn't mean she won't advocate for Wailea Chapel...it's where she and our father were married, it's where we were all baptized, it's where Katie and I were both married. Mom attends Sunday services at Wailea Chapel."

"And it's where Dad's funeral was held," Shane said solemnly.

Ah, she hadn't thought of that. Shane always acted like he didn't absorb the hard things in life. He seemed to be able to rise above hurts and grab the fun and joy in life. Despite hiding the fact, their father's passing no doubt had hit him hard.

"I think if you are direct and just tell Mom that, she'll completely understand. It's still early...not even a year since we lost him."

Shane drew a deep breath of relief. "Yeah, you're right. I'll just tell her. She'll understand."

"Of course, she may suggest Pali Maui as an alternative," Christel warned.

Shane leaned back in his chair. "Yeah. But she's also a softy. If I tell her we want to be supportive of Halia and Kina, she'll fold easily, don't you think? I mean, that's why I'm here. I want to make sure you agree that I won't hurt Mom's feelings if I stick with Banana Patch."

Christel nodded. True, their mother always said people mattered more than things. She was sure their mother would be supportive of Aimee and Shane's choice of wedding venues for that reason. "I think you have nothing to worry about, Shane."

Her brother looked relieved. "What about you?" he asked.

"Me? What do you mean?" Christel wrapped up the uneaten half of the burger, now cold. She pushed it aside, along with the remaining fries.

"When are you and Evan going to walk the aisle?"

The question caught Christel off guard. "Why are you asking?" she posed, stalling.

Shane's face broke into a grin and he shrugged. "Well, you've been dating for a while now. A guy who's willing to carry you off a mountain is a potential candidate for making a life partner, don't you think?"

She thought her little brother's criteria for picking her future husband was a little off, and she told him so. "I'm sure you asked Aimee to marry you for deeper reasons."

Again, her little brother shrugged. "Well, yeah. Aimee's hot, she's really nice to look at, and we have fun. But the biggest thing? She's my baby's mother. That was the decision point." He saw the look on Christel's face, and continued. "Don't get me wrong, I really love her and all. But I have my own family now. I want to be an important part of Carson's life, and Aimee's. I want to teach the kid to surf, to love Star Wars, and all the lines to get the girls...when he gets old enough. The thought of someone else in that role really needles me, you know?"

Yes, she did know. She was reluctant to move forward with her relationship with Evan, unsure if she was truly over the demise of her first marriage. It wasn't fair to bring that baggage into the mix. Yet, thinking of Evan with anyone but her...Well, she had a hard time imagining it without feeling immense pain. She supposed that was a clue that she was in love with him. Yes, she knew that. Had known it for some time. Yet, in some small way, she still loved Jay. Always would.

What exactly was she supposed to do with that?

"I know what you mean, Shane. I do," she admitted. "Sometimes, though, other factors are at play. I've learned to act on what's best...not just what I feel."

Shane rolled his eyes. "You're just scared."

His accusation bit. "I'm not scared," she argued. "I'm simply a little wiser than I once was. This isn't my first carnival. I've ridden the Ferris wheel and eaten the cotton candy."

"This isn't a carnival, Christel. This is life," he told her. "Besides, you miss out on a lot when you won't buckle up for the hairy rides."

She was surprised at his wisdom. Seems Shane had matured overnight." Where'd you get all this insight?" she asked.

"Are you kidding me?" He laughed. "I grew up with two older sisters."

"What about your brother?" she teased. "Don't leave him out."

"Aiden's far too serious...and I'm not sure he's an authority on marriage, and all. He's never even been in an earnest relationship, at least not that I know of." He pushed the remainder of his hamburger into his mouth and paused to chew before continuing. "Aiden did teach me to catch a mean wave and ride it all the way in. I guess you could say my passion for surfing is greater than my fear of sharks." He looked her directly in the eye. "Caution is overrated, Christel. Especially if it makes you miss the ride of your life."

19

"Willa, honey. Come on out...please?" Katie rapped on her daughter's closed bedroom door a second time. "Let's talk."

"There's nothing to talk about," came a muffled reply. "My life is ruined. You can't fix that."

Katie felt her heart plunge. "I'm not going to try to fix it, Willa. I just want to talk." Despite the lack of invitation, she gently pushed the door and peeked inside. There was her precious daughter, crumpled on top of her bed. Wadded tissues were piled on the floor, along with an empty box. Another box was wedged in the bedcovers, close to Willa.

Her daughter grabbed a tissue from the box and blew her nose. "What do you want?" she asked miserably between blows.

"Honey, we need to talk." Katie had thought it reasonable to allow Willa to stay home from school, especially since she'd slept or sobbed on and off the day following the incident. Over the past twenty-four hours, every time her daughter picked up her phone, she'd moan out loud. She checked her laptop several times and each time nearly put her over the top. Despite

Amanda's attempt to remove the pictures, they'd taken on a life of their own.

It appeared everyone had indeed seen the photograph. For the first twenty-four hours, texts and messages flooded Willa's inbox and phone, some supportive but far more were mean and candidly cruel in nature. Some of the football players were the worst. The police were involved now, sending warning messages to every kid who had reposted—letting them know passing on the vicious photos was a criminal act.

Katie had Willa's passwords and had printed the worst ones, intending to hand them off to the school counselor in their meeting today. Even beyond what her daughter had suffered, the quickness of these kids to jump on the bandwagon was frightening. Something should be done. This kind of badgering should be addressed. Especially given the words these kids used, seemingly without flinching.

Finally, it appeared as though the offending photographs of Willa and Kina had been removed from all sources—at least no one was reposting.

Katie sat on the edge of the bed. "Baby, I wish I could make all this go away. Unfortunately, I'm not able to make all this better, so we need a plan...a strategy for you to deal with this so you can return to school. You can't just stay in your bedroom."

Willa shook her head miserably and sniffed. "Are you kidding? I'm never going to school again! Never! You can homeschool me." She buried her face into her pillow and sobbed. "Did you read those messages? The names they are calling me?"

Katie had never seen Willa this undone. Her daughter was typically strong-natured and reluctant to buy into drama...at school or anywhere else. But this was personal. The idea of people gawking at a nearly naked torso and believing it was her was more than Willa could bear.

Willa rolled over, swiped her forearm across her blotched

face. "One guy—anonymous, of course—asked me out and detailed the things he'd like to do once we were alone."

Katie ached inside. Never had she felt so helpless...or so angry. This stunt had shattered Willa's spirit to bits. It was her job to glue her fragile daughter back together.

Sadly, she had little idea how to pull her girl out of this.

It was Aiden who came up with a possible solution. "Go talk to the school counselor," he advised. "They are good at this stuff. There are all kinds of special training programs they've been through. Surely, the counselors will know how to help Willa navigate the fallout."

Katie looked up at him, thankful. "You're right," she said. "Thanks, Aiden." She leaned and brushed a kiss across her brother's cheek.

Katie showed up at the counselor's office later that afternoon, thinking there was no better time than now to deal with this mess.

"Come in," the counselor told her, waving her inside the tiny office, a tight little room lined with bookshelves filled with college catalogs and FAFSA publications.

"Thanks for taking the time to see me," Katie said, taking a seat. At the same time, the counselor returned to her own chair behind a badly marred walnut desk.

The woman gave her a warm smile. "I'm Barrie Graeber. What can I do to help?"

Katie had done her research. Barrie Graeber had joined the staff at Maui High School only last year after a distinguished career on the speaking circuit. From what Katie had read, Ms. Graeber had a real heart for teens, a result of a personal tragedy she'd endured with her own daughter while living in Idaho.

Katie took a deep breath and explained the entire story, leaving nothing out. Ms. Graeber couldn't help unless she understood everything that had happened. She handed her a stack of printed emails and texts, even a few horrible photos that had been sent to her daughter in the aftermath of Amanda's prank.

"I'm really worried about Willa," Katie confided. "She won't get out of bed. She claims she's never returning to school. I know this is awful, but Willa is often resilient. This just isn't like her."

Ms. Graeber nodded with sympathy. "I'm glad you came to me. You see, I'm a strong believer that we think these kids are stronger than they are. It's always wise to take these behaviors seriously." She shared her own story. Her daughter's name was Pearl. She suffered a betrayal that sent her spiraling. In the aftermath, she'd acted out in ways that were completely incongruent with her nature. She took chances and made decisions that ultimately led to a car accident that took her life.

"I don't share this story to scare you," she confided. "I do want to assure you that your concern is warranted." She smiled at Katie. "And that you don't have to do this alone. I understand, and I'm here to help both you and Willa."

Simply knowing she and Jon didn't have to shoulder this alone, especially with their limited knowledge about dealing with cyber bullying and matters like this...well, it gave her courage to face the situation head-on. She'd do everything she could to make this right for her daughter.

"If you're comfortable with the idea, I'd like to meet with Willa as soon as possible. Until then, I will alert the rest of the counseling staff and we'll have a group think. Some of the best solutions form when we all put our brains together."

WILLA RELUCTANTLY MET with Barrie Graeber early the next morning, prior to the first bell at school.

"Do you want to share with me what's going on?" Ms. Graeber gently asked.

"Didn't my mom tell you?" Her eyes teared up and she looked at the floor.

"Yes, but I want to hear your take on it. I want to know how this is making *you* feel." She handed a tissue across the desk.

It took some prodding, but finally Willa recounted the entire saga, starting with how Amanda used to be her friend. She told her about the pregnancy test in the trash, how her dad thought the wand with the pink line was hers. When Amanda was told what had happened to Willa, she brushed it off. "She didn't seem to care that my parents suspected me."

"Oh, Willa. That's awful. What happened then?" Ms. Graeber urged.

Willa explained how Amanda's mother took her to the mainland and that she'd returned to Maui no longer pregnant.

Ms. Graeber showed no emotion. She simply nodded.

Willa went on to confide that Amanda became one of *those* girls.

"Those girls?" Ms. Graeber asked with lifted brows.

Willa nodded. "The mean girl. She struts down the hallway in her two-hundred-dollar outfits and makes life living hell for anyone who is unwilling to worship at her feet." She had a few other choice words for describing Amanda Cooper but thought it best to keep those to herself.

Ms. Graeber looked across the desk. "Is that what bothers you most?"

Willa thought a minute. She shook her head. "No. What bothers me most is that she hurts people."

"She hurt you," Ms. Graeber stated.

"Yes, and she hurt Kina."

Ms. Graeber took a deep breath. "Well, that's what bothers me the most, too. I want you to know you are not alone in this. Your parents, your extended family, and me...we're all on your side and are going to walk this with you." She paused as if contemplating whether or not to share more. Finally, she continued. "I reached out to Amanda's mother. It appears this situation is going to come to a close quickly. You will likely not be facing this issue with Amanda again."

Willa's eyebrows shot up. "Why's that?"

"Amanda's mother is recently engaged. She and Amanda are moving to Denver, Colorado, to live with her mom's new fiancé."

"Moving?" Willa was stunned.

"Yes, Amanda withdrew from Maui High this morning." At the relieved look on Willa's face, Ms. Graeber continued. "I know that doesn't erase the photos. But it does mean there will not be any future incidents with the Cooper girl." She gave Willa an encouraging smile from across the desk.

"Not for you...and not for Kina."

20

"Man, this place is dope!" Shane scanned the open interior of the Banana Patch, with wooden walls draped with bright-colored fabrics and pots of lush plants decorating the corners of the room. Open sliders revealed a view of ponds surrounded by banana palms and hibiscus. "Wow, Aunt Vanessa was right. This is exactly what we were looking for."

Aimee linked her arm in his. "See? I told you."

Suddenly, a strange voice repeated what she'd said. "See? I told you." A parrot squawked.

They both turned to find a large bird with feathers of red, orange, yellow, and blue. "I told you. I told you," the parrot repeated, bobbing its head up and down.

Shane laughed. Before he could say anything, the parrot started up again. "Knock, knock."

Aimee grinned. "Who's there?" she said, playing along.

The bird squawked. "Who's there? Who's there? A parrot."

"A parrot who?" Shane asked.

"A-parrot-ly, some birds can talk!"

Amid their laughter, Halia swept into the room, wearing a

caftan, and her long brown hair wrapped in a turban. "I see you've met Coconut."

Aimee greeted her with a wave. "Yes, we did. Your parrot friend is a riot."

"Yeah," Shane agreed. "And quite the comedian."

"I'm glad you think so. Perhaps we could arrange for Coconut to officiate your ceremony," Haila offered, teasing. "Then again, your mom might not appreciate going with that choice."

A smile wiggled at the edges of Shane's mouth. "I suppose not," he agreed. "A parrot marrying us would definitely put her over the top."

Aimee gently elbowed him. "Oh, stop. Your mom has been very supportive, even when we diverted from her preferred plans."

Over the next hour, Aimee and Shane followed Halia through the grounds and discussed all the options before them. After considering multiple places for the actual ceremony to take place, eventually, they landed on a spot in front of the serenity pond.

The water was shallow and lined with a large stone patio and walkway. There was plenty of room for chairs. They heartily agreed when Halia suggested they surround the entire area with candles and lit torches. The ceremony would take place at dusk, and she said the ambience would be stunning.

"It's perfect," Aimee said, clasping her hands together and smiling widely. "Just perfect."

Shane grinned over at his fiancée. He loved it when she was this happy.

21

Christel slid into the corner booth at Charley's next to her brother, Aiden. "Sorry I'm late everyone."

"No worries. I was late, too. Just not as late as you," Katie teased.

Christel grabbed one of the plastic menus off the table. "I'm starving." She quickly perused the selections, then glanced around. "Where's Shane?"

Aiden tilted his head in the direction of a nearby table where Aimee was passing out glasses of water. "Aimee's working, so he has baby duty today."

Christel's eyebrows lifted. "I thought they'd lined up childcare."

Katie grabbed a napkin and wiped the moisture from the outside her water glass. "Apparently, the little guy isn't feeling well. He was sniffling last night and Shane thought it best that he stayed home with Carson today."

Christel nodded. "Ah...makes sense." She closed her menu and placed it on the table. "Seems it's getting harder and harder to get us all here each week." *Here* was a popular bar and restaurant named Charley's, where graybeard bikers and young surfers lined up for the best food and fun around. The Briscoe siblings had been gathering at Charley's for over three years. The regular lunch dates were their time to connect...just the four of them.

Katie shrugged. "Well, I get it. I've been a parent for years, and I still struggle to make time for myself. It's especially hard when they are babies."

"Yeah, Shane is new to this. He'll get it all figured out," Aiden offered in support of his younger brother. "It's not like Shane ever passes up a good time intentionally."

"True," Katie agreed.

Aimee spotted them from across the room and waved. Minutes later, she made her way over to their table. "Hey, how's it going?"

Katie gave her future sister-in-law a wide smile. "Looks like they're keeping you busy." She glanced around at the crowded tables. "It's really packed today."

Aimee pulled her order pad from her pocket and shrugged. "That means lots of tips. Shane and I can use every extra dollar right now. What with buying the house and all."

"How's the real estate deal coming along?" Aiden asked her.

"Shane says we close in two weeks, just before the wedding."

Katie couldn't hide her excitement. "If you need any help, just let me know. I'd love to assist in the decorating. I know from experience that there are a lot of details with weddings, and you may find yourself running short on time. I could even help with the wedding, if you need. You don't want anything to slip through the cracks and cause stress. I mean, it's your special day and you'll want everything to go perfectly."

Aimee pulled a pen from behind her ear and clicked it open. "I think we're good. We're keeping everything really simple."

"Oh, yeah...sure," Katie said. "But, if you change your mind, just holler. We'd all love to help in any way possible." She looked around the table. "Right?"

Christel and Aiden nodded in agreement before turning their attention to their menus. Poor Katie. She seemed lost now that her house was built and they'd moved in. It wouldn't be long before she landed on another project. That was her sister's *modus operandi*.

Aimee took their orders, noting Katie's request to hold the pickles from her hamburger and Aiden's quick offer to have his sister's pickles dumped on his plate.

"What?" he said when all of them looked his way. "I like pickles."

Christel gathered the menus and handed them off to Aimee. "We were just talking about you and Shane and about how difficult it must be to juggle the parenting duties."

"Yeah, about that. Sorry your brother had to stay home with Carson. I told him he should just bring the baby with him. He's no trouble, really. I mean, we can't just put our lives on hold because we've got a kid."

Christel reached for her water glass. "They say ninety percent of parenting is just thinking about when you can lay down again."

A wistful look crossed Aimee's face. "Yeah, true. Parenting changes everything."

Katie nodded in agreement. "The biggest thing I remember about the early weeks is that there was no transition. Both Jon and I had to hit the ground diapering."

They all laughed.

"Well, I'll get these orders in. Peace out." Aimee turned and headed for the kitchen.

"Peace out?" Christel said, her voice lowered.

"I think Aimee's been spending too much time at the Banana Patch with Halia," Katie offered. "If she starts wearing long skirts and smelling like patchouli, we may have to do an intervention before we allow her in the family."

Aiden leaned back against the red vinyl banquette. "Like you could ever stop Shane from marrying her. I mean, that boy is crazy in love."

"I know, right?" Christel asked. "The way he ogles Aimee is right out of that scene in *Bambi*. That cute little skunk has nothing on Shane when it comes to being twitterpated."

Katie picked up the salt shaker and wiped it with her napkin. "I think it's sweet." She turned to Aiden. "One brother down. One to go."

Their brother swallowed a groan and held up his hands in protest. "Whoa. Let's not go there. I'm married to my job right now. That's about all I can handle at the moment."

"Yeah, about that. How's everything going?" Christel asked him. "What's happening at the station?"

Aiden shrugged. "Being captain isn't so different than my old job. I still do all the same things, only now I make all the critical decisions and have everybody coming to me with their complaints." He let out a chuckle. "Last week, a guy who transferred in from Honolulu took issue with the number of urinals in the bathroom. Apparently, he can't hold it until one of the two becomes available."

Christel shoulder bumped her brother. "The bane of becoming the boss, eh?"

"You worked hard to get there," Katie gently reminded. "You know what Dad used to pound into us...leadership comes with responsibility. They are lucky to have you at the helm."

They all sat silent for several seconds. It wasn't often any of them made mention of their father. The memories were still too fresh...too painful.

Finally, Aiden broke the silence. "Thanks, Sis," he muttered a bit sarcastically. "I hope I can live up to everyone's expectations."

Ignoring the tone in her brother's voice, Christel folded her hands on the table and decided to change the subject. "What about that girl who was giving you a hard time?"

Aiden hesitated a moment before replying. "You mean Meghan McCord?"

"Yeah, the girl with the tiger tattoo. What's going on with her these days?"

Aiden's returning laugh lacked humor. "She's started dating some guy. He stops by the station on occasion. Can't say I care for him much."

"Yeah? Why's that?" Katie asked.

"He's what I call a *globehead*," Aiden told his sisters. "Ron Culvane thinks the whole world revolves around him, know what I mean? The other day, the guy stopped by the station to pick Meghan up and drive her home—her car was in the shop for a tune-up—and he got all out of sorts when he discovered she wasn't there to meet him like they'd planned. I mean, search and rescue workers can't exactly schedule how long they're out on a call. So, this guy walks around the station muttering about how inconsiderate she's being. He keeps checking his watch and his expression becomes more and more sour with every passing minute." Aiden rubbed at his chin. "We offer the guy a seat and a cup of coffee while he waits. He barely responds. Finally, he huffs out of the station." Aiden shook his head. "Less than ten minutes later, Meghan shows back up at the station and doesn't have a ride home. So, I take her. When we pull up to her house, he's there waiting in his car, which is parked in her driveway. I mean, weird."

Katie frowned. "Goodness! Where did she meet him?"

"At the gym. Apparently, Meghan signed up for a weightlifting class and he's the instructor."

Christel's face sobered and she stated the obvious. "She'd better be careful. He sounds like a creep."

Aiden fingered his fork. "Well, Meghan's tough. She can

hold her own. I doubt she'll put up with him long if he keeps this act up."

Aimee returned to the table, juggling plates of food on her arms. "Here you go," she said as she placed the orders in front of them. "Katie, here's your hamburger, sans pickles. Aiden, your turkey sandwich, extra pickles."

"Extra pickles?" Christel exclaimed. "That's a small mountain on that plate."

Aimee winked. "Perks of being almost family." She placed Christel's salad before her, then grabbed a ketchup bottle from her apron pocket and set it on the table. "Well, let me know if you need anything else."

When their future sister-in-law had retreated back to the kitchen, Aiden poked a pickle slice in his mouth and looked across the table as he reached for another. "So, Katie. How's Willa?"

"My girl's still hurting," she admitted. "I know it's only been a couple of days, but I'd hoped meeting with the counselor and all would help move our daughter past this incident. Especially when she learned the threat is over."

"Over?" Aiden asked.

"Amanda Cooper's mother is engaged again and they are leaving the island."

Christel stabbed some lettuce with her fork. "Good riddance!" Well aware her response was a bit harsh, she quickly added, "These things take time, I suppose."

Katie readily agreed. "Especially for young teenagers. Truthfully, I've never felt so inept at helping my daughter. Nothing we say or do seems to help. She can't seem to shake the shame of it all."

Aiden's eyes grew serious. "Maybe you should take a family vacation. A change of scenery might do her good."

"I wish we could," Katie said. "Jon's sous chef just informed him he was going to be needing some minor surgery and will be away from work for a while. Jon will be shouldering more duties than normal in the coming weeks." She shook her head. "We simply need a fix. Unfortunately, none of us seems to know what that might be."

KATIE WALKED into her front door still thinking about Willa and how she might help her daughter move past the cyberbullying. She couldn't argue and tell her heartbroken daughter that the entire school hadn't seen those photos. Likely, they had. So had the teachers. No amount of explaining that the photographs were digitally manufactured, that the images were not authentic, could erase the damage those images had created.

Frankly, it was surprising that anyone who knew her daughter really believed those images were Willa. She would never strike those poses, and in so few clothes.

Katie blamed social media...and television. The lack of appropriate boundaries in current entertainment venues, and the influence those salacious acts had on young people's minds, created a surreal belief that all of America had slipped into a pit of debauchery.

Katie pulled a deep breath. There were still kids who would not succumb to that garbage...namely her daughter, Willa. And, her friend, Kina. Hopefully, there were others.

Katie did not necessarily view herself as a prude, but did celebrities really need to undulate in a sexual manner on stage...even during a televised football halftime? That kind of dancing was better kept behind closed doors, perhaps in Vegas, where children would not be exposed to suggestive things they were not ready to see.

Those influences, together with a lack of parental supervision and training, opened doors to what Amanda Cooper had done. She had no filter, no empathy. She believed posting those soul-crushing photos was funny.

It wasn't.

Katie turned to find Jon walking in the door. "Hi, babe." He greeted her with a kiss to the cheek.

She pointed to the apron he was still wearing. "Busy day?"

"And then some. I just came home to check on Willa, and then I have to return to the restaurant. We have a wedding party coming in later tonight."

Katie sighed. "Well, I guess we'll eat without you then." Unfortunately, Jon was missing from their dinner table more and more lately. She made note to take Aiden up on his suggestion and plan a getaway for their family as soon as Jon's workload lightened up. A vacation would do all of them good.

Her husband picked up Noelle. He playfully rubbed his nose with hers. "Where's sissy?" he asked her.

She pointed to the stairs. "Willa up 'dare."

He kissed the top of the little girl's head and set her down. "You stay here, Noelle. I'm going to go check on her."

Katie watched him climb the stairs, a father with a mission. He was as distraught as she over Willa's heartbreak. They'd both been worried sick and were beginning to wonder if their daughter would ever fully recover. Oh, they knew she would eventually. Still, the event had marred Willa's spirit. She'd no doubt carry a memory of this hurt with her always.

Katie checked her watch, deciding to pull a frozen lasagna out of the freezer...Willa's favorite. After pulling back the aluminum cover to vent the steam, Katie slid the container onto a baking sheet and placed it into her new oven. She set the timer.

Unfortunately, when it was time to sit down and eat, her daughter claimed she wasn't hungry, leaving most of the lasagna left over. Katie wrapped the pan with aluminum foil and placed it in the refrigerator.

Willa looked up from the table where she was leaning over an open math book. "Mom?"

"Yeah, baby?"

"Ms. Graeber at school says Amanda and those girls were feeling inadequate and were seeking out attention. She says I'm only a victim if I choose to be."

Katie hoped none of her apprehension showed in her voice. "I think Ms. Graeber gave wise counsel." There was more she wanted to say, but inside she knew this time less was more. What her daughter really needed right now was a safe place to share her feelings.

"Did you know that Ms. Graeber lost her daughter in a car accident?"

"Yes, she shared that with your dad and me."

"Yeah, Ms. Graeber knows how it feels to hurt inside. She understands a lot. I really like her."

"I'm really glad, sweetheart." This was what Katie had been counting on, that a well-trained counselor would gain her daughter's trust and give her hope that this incident would not wreck her life.

"Mom?"

"Yeah, babe?"

"Do you think the kids at school will ever like me again?"

The question caused Katie's heart to fold in on itself. The thing paramount in her daughter's mind was the shake-up in her social status at school. Kids that age cared immensely how their peers viewed them. They wanted to be popular more than eat.

Katie folded her daughter into her arms and kissed the top of her hair. "Yes, baby. I truly believe you'll have all the friends you want." She stopped at reminding Willa the students who stooped to Amanda's level were not her friends anyway.

Over the next minutes, Katie held her daughter, admittedly tickled her daughter allowed her to do so. How long had it been? When Willa was Noelle's age, she would climb onto Katie's lap and say, "Mommy, hold me a little bit of time."

Back then, she loved cuddles and being held. As the years passed, so had her daughter's tolerance for physical affection... especially from her parents. In Willa's mind, she was far too old for any of that.

Outside, Katie could see it was getting dark. She brushed another kiss on top of Willa's head. "Why don't you go take a hot bath, baby. I'll even let you use my tub and some of those fancy bath bombs we now carry in the gift shop. Use one of the lavender-scented ones."

Willa closed her math book. "Can I fix a snack first?"

Katie wanted to remind her daughter she hadn't eaten any dinner, yet quickly made the decision to let the matter go. "Sure, honey. There's a stash of peanut butter cups hidden behind the cereal boxes in the pantry." She winked, delighted at the smile that brought to Willa's face.

Her phone rang and Katie headed for the counter and picked it up. "Hi, Mom. What's up?"

"You may want to look outside," her mother advised. "And Willa, too."

Puzzled, Katie motioned to Willa. "Nana says we need to go to the window." She motioned for her daughter to follow. She moved for the windows. It didn't take a lot of effort, given the whole front of their new home was glass.

Suddenly, Katie's breath caught. "Willa, hurry. Come see."

Outside, a large crowd of kids had assembled. They held lit candles in the air.

22

Shane finished feeding Carson and placed the empty bottle on the sofa table. "Hey, Aimee," he hollered. "You ready? The real estate lady should be here any moment."

When his fiancée failed to answer, Shane placed Carson in his Pack 'n Play and wandered back to the bedroom. Aimee was on the bed scrolling through her phone, like she did for hours every night. "You haven't even showered! Wimberly Ann will be here any minute."

Aimee rolled her eyes. "Settle down, will you? I showered this morning."

He refrained from telling her she smelled like the grill at Charlie's. "Yeah, okay. Well, she'll be here soon."

She stood. "I'll brush my hair and throw some DKNY perfume on. Will that do?" she teased.

He nodded. Once she'd retreated to the bathroom, Shane glanced down at her phone on the bed. He knew he shouldn't, but the draw was intense. His eyes darted around the room, then back at the bathroom door. Now he could hear water running.

Curious as to why Aimee spent so much time scrolling through her phone, he quickly picked it up and clicked on it. Pushing guilt aside, he let his eyes scan the tiny screen. The browser was open to a Hollywood casting site."

"Are you snooping on my phone?"

His heart seized and he quit breathing. Slowly, he turned with the phone still in his hand. "Uh, no," he managed to say.

Aimee laughed. She took the phone from his hand. "Lighten up, Shane. Geez! I don't care if you look at my phone. Nothing there I'm hiding."

Shane felt his cheeks pinken. "I—well, what was that casting call page? I mean, you're not returning to California, are you?" Even as he pushed the words from his mouth, his throat constricted with fear.

"Of course not, silly." She gave his shoulder a playful shove. "Why would I book it now when we're about to buy a really cool house. Plus, we're a family now...right?"

Relief flooded every cell of Shane's body. "Yeah, yeah...we're a family. I was silly to even think you might leave again." He pulled her into his arms. "I just love you, you know? I couldn't stand the thought of anything changing. I'm so happy right now."

"Me, too," she promised.

That was his cue.

Shane pulled Aimee closer, holding her against him. She smelled like a mixture of flowers and oranges. One hand rose to her jaw. He lifted her face and he went after her mouth like a starving man. He buried his other hand in her long, blonde hair, enjoying the silky feel. He groaned against her mouth, and she let out a little moan of her own.

The doorbell rang, startling them both back to the present.

"Guess she's here," Aimee said, straightening her T-shirt.

"Uh, yeah." Shane ran a hand through his hair, grabbed his fiancée's hand. Together, they made their way to the front door where they greeted Wimberly Ann. She wore a tight pair of black leather pants and an off-the-shoulder sweater in a light shade of yellow. Large earrings dangled from her ears and a stack of bangle bracelets made noise as the jewelry clinked together on her wrist.

"Hey, you two! Ready to buy a house?" She held up a large stack of documents, many of them fastened together with little black clips. "These are your closing documents. I want you to review them before tomorrow, when we meet at the escrow office. I've put notes and highlighted all the places where you'll be signing in front of a notary."

Shane's eyes widened. "Boy, that's a lot of paper."

Wimberly Ann grinned. "Oh, honey. Don't let none of that scare you. It's just standard legal mumbo-jumbo. Don't worry about a thing. Wimberly Ann has you all set and ready to go." She gave them both a reassuring look. "By this time tomorrow, you'll have keys in hand."

"Uh, is it okay if my sister looks these over too? Christel's an attorney and has her CPA license."

"Of course, darlin'. She's welcome to offer any advice she deems necessary. Although, I will warn that these are standard form documents. I've used them, or ones like them, hundreds of times."

Shane and Aimee exchanged glances. Aimee had a wide grin on her face.

Shane let himself smile as well as he squeezed his fiancée's hand. "Sounds like we'll be homeowners soon."

MIG PULLED up to the offices in his prized Chevy Bel Air and cut the engine. He climbed out and shut the driver's door, taking a moment to rub a spot of dirt with his sleeve.

"Yoo hoo! Mr. Nakamoa?"

He turned to find that realtor lady walking in his direction. She wore pants that hugged her frame and a shirt that showed off cleavage. She also wore a look of determination.

"Mr. Nakamoa? I mean, Miguel...can I call you that? Or better, how about Miggy. I'll call you Miggy."

He cringed at the presumptuous nickname. "Friends calls me Mig," he informed her.

She looped her arm through the crook of his elbow. "Well, I hope we're friends." Her eyes suddenly widened. "Oh, my goodness! That car!" She glanced back at him with a look of amazement. "Is that a '55?"

She reached and stroked the hood like it was a cat. "Red and white is my favorite paint job that year. Actually, the factory colors are Gypsy Red and India Ivory. Sea Mist Green is a close second, in terms of favorites, but, oh...this car is like chocolate pudding to a starving man."

Bending, she examined the wide white sidewall tires and rear wheel skirts. "Topped with a dollop of whipped cream," she added.

Mig couldn't help but appreciate the view. Speaking of starving men, it had been more than a little while since he last felt his heart speed up because of a woman's backside. She was a bit bold—over the top, really—but her curves made up for that.

"You like cars?" he asked, watching as she straightened.

"Like cars? Honey, it's been reported that when I was a tiny kid, I passed up Barbies for Matchbox cars every time. When other girls were picking out prom dresses, I was on my knees praying to the good Lord that Tommy Bennett would ask me to the dance, just so I could ride in his aqua Corvette." Reverence appeared on her face. "Truth was, I'd dance with the devil to slip into those leather seats."

Mig felt himself warming to the woman. Not only was she a looker, she possessed a rare love of cars. That was a trait you just didn't find in many females.

23

Ava wandered the path under the landmark banyan tree in Lahaina, heading in the direction of her brother's boat slip on the boardwalk. She was plenty early, as was her tendency, which allowed her to take her time and enjoy the familiar sights.

A mother was kneeling with her camera poised, trying to get the perfect shot of her husband and four small children. One of the kids, a little boy, broke from where they were posed when a rooster darted in front of them. He chased the bird, running as fast as his little legs would take him. "Mark," the mother called. "You get back here, right now!"

Ava smiled to herself. She remembered those days when much of her time and energy went to corralling her own four. Christel and Aiden could be counted on to obey her instructions while Katie and Shane's attention was easily diverted. Life was too short for them to follow her rules...a fact that caused a rise in Lincoln's blood pressure.

She sighed, realizing it had been weeks since thoughts of her late husband passed through her mind. Lincoln had been dead less than a year yet it often felt like a lifetime ago when she'd stood next to his casket in Wailea Chapel. The tiny piece of paper she discovered in his suit pocket that day was the beginning of a heartbreak she never saw coming.

Ava lifted her chin. She had survived—both his passing and his betrayal. Not an easy feat, but a testament to the power of intention. Her brother, Jack, had urged her to take control of her life and her emotions. Not to discount the pain, but she was a victim only if she elected to be one. She had slipped off the hurt and instead donned joy.

It was a choice. One she was glad she'd made.

In the aftermath, she'd had to learn to fill her time with things that made her happy. She tried new adventures, like the time spent at the Banana Patch spa. She discovered yoga was not her thing, yet the peace in the surrounding garden had filled her soul.

She could understand why Shane and Aimee might choose to be married in such a place. She even found herself admiring how they'd shed themselves of others' expectations and planned a simple ceremony, one designed to reflect their own special relationship. Shane had arranged to stand at the front with Carson in his arms as Aimee made her way down the aisle. The way her son viewed things, the day was not only a marriage, but a melding of a family.

Ava didn't often wish she could still speak to Lincoln, but if the occasion somehow arose, she'd relish telling him she was right about Shane. He wasn't a foolish and lazy kid who was reluctant to grow up. Yes, he lived life to its fullest, but their son had stepped up and embraced responsibility without a snag. She always sensed that inside of him.

Jack was sitting on an overturned bucket on the deck next to his boat. "There you are," he said, as Ava approached. He stood and kissed her cheek. "You're looking good, Sister."

She patted his ample belly. "You too, Brother."

Jack buttoned up his shirt until only some black chest hair

peeked out. "Well, where are we going? This is your show. Are we going to try some new restaurant? Don't make it too fancy," he warned. "I haven't showered in a few days."

She poked him with her elbow, knowing he was teasing. "We're going to the swap meet in Kahului."

"Swap meet, eh? Sounds good to me."

Ava gave her brother a warm smile. "You just want some warm malasadas."

"What's wrong with that?" he asked as he followed her.

The Maui Swap Meet in Kahului had been an institution loved by both residents and tourists since the early nineteen eighties. Held every Saturday morning, people flocked to the flea-market-type venue to discover local crafts and foods at bargain prices.

Once parked, Ava and Jack made their way to the admission booth. Jack pulled out his wallet from his pocket and handed a dollar bill to the lady behind the small window. "Keep the change," he said, laughing and knowing admission was a mere fifty cents each. For good measure, he pulled a twenty and handed it over. "And here's a little something for being so nice."

Jack was like that. Her brother was a brute of a man who looked very much like Santa Claus in a beach shirt and surfer shorts and was soft as sugar cookie dough in the middle.

He shoved his wallet back in place. "Well, where to first?"

Ava scanned the rows of vendor booths in the distance. "Let's start over there." She pointed to the first row to the left.

Together, Ava and Jack progressed along the wide paved walkway lined with brightly colored banners flapping in the breeze coming in off the ocean. Overhead, an airplane cut through the blue sky, leaving a white jet stream in its wake.

Jack rubbed at his belly. "Smells durn good."

Ava arched her eyebrows. "So, you're telling me you want to hit the malasada booth first?"

"I'm buying," he told her.

Everyone knew Portuguese malasadas were best served scorching hot. The yeast dough was close to a donut's in texture, springy inside and crisp on the outside. They were stuffed with a variety of pudding-like fillings, deep-fried, and then rolled in sugar.

The tented booth was only a few feet away. A hand-printed paper banner was fastened to the top corners of a bright blue awning. A woman with dark skin and gray hair wiped her hands on her apron. "How many?" she asked, grabbing a box made of Styrofoam. With her other hand, she grabbed a pair of silver tongs and held them in mid-air, waiting.

"Make mine a mango cheesecake rolled in powdered sugar," he told her with a wide smile.

Ava followed with her order. "Haupia coconut with cinnamon." She paused and looked at the menu board. "And a coffee."

The woman lifted an elbow and rubbed away a stray piece of gray hair with her forearm. "Gotcha. Coming right up."

She handed over the box and cup of coffee. Jack paid. Before they exited the booth, Jack leaned over the counter. "These little balls of love don't have anything on how sweet you've been this morning." He winked in her direction.

His attention caused her mouth to break into a wide grin, showing off a missing tooth.

Ava smiled over at her brother. Jack never ceased being the charmer.

As they moseyed along the row of booths, she bit into her malasada and moaned with pleasure.

"Worth the trip right there," Jack claimed as he did the same. Two bites later, he was finished. Ava offered him her second one.

"Nah, I can't. That's yours," he told her with hands raised in protest.

"Of course, you can," she argued, pushing the box into his chest. "It's our routine."

"You're right." He grinned and popped the entire malasada in his mouth.

They spent the next hours inspecting tropical print bags and dresses, handmade soap and artisan jewelry. There were booths that sold freshly cut herbs and local fruits, including dragon fruits, avocados, mangos, and pineapples.

Ava purchased a large bundle of bok choy. She loved the mild, cabbage-like flavor of the vegetable sauteed with lemon, garlic, and soy sauce.

"How's that little granddaughter of yours?" Jack asked. "I was sure sorry to hear of that ordeal. Kids can be so mean."

Ava told him how she'd been horrified that some mean girl at school had distributed those photos in retribution of Willa standing up against their bullying of her new friend, Kina. Despite how hard the incident had been on them all, it had ended well. "Yes, there are bullies," she conceded. "But there are also really good-hearted kids." She told her brother how Willa's classmates had gathered outside her house holding lit candles. The showing of solidarity was just what was needed to lift Willa from her slump and allowed her to return to her old self. Katie had even heard her in her bedroom talking on the phone and giggling, just like before.

She told him about the upcoming wedding plans and made sure he'd circled the date on the calendar. "The big day is in less than two weeks," she warned. "We want you there to help us celebrate."

"I wouldn't miss it," he assured her.

"Sounds like everything is going well, Sis," he said, stopping to pick up a scrimshaw pocket knife. It had a handle crafted of carved bone with hand-etched nautical themes, including clipper ships and whales.

"You want that?" Ava asked. Not bothering to wait for his

reply, she pulled a few bills from her purse and handed them to the booth's proprietor.

"Ava, you didn't have to do that," he protested.

She drew her brother into a shoulder hug. "Yes, I did." She winked. "It's our routine."

24

Aiden signed the last purchase order of the day and placed it on the stack to the side of his desk. While the promotion to captain was an honor, he had to admit the added administrative duties were not his favorite part of the job. Unfortunately, those responsibilities took up over half his time.

He stood and made his way to the kitchen, hoping to find a box of crackers. He was hungry and wanted to grab a snack to tide him over until he joined his mom for dinner.

Aiden made his way to the stairway and descended, taking two stairs at a time. Sitting for so many hours was not his friend. Every chance for a little exercise was a gift. The guys ribbed him all the time about being a desk bunny. They teased he'd get soft sitting at that desk for hours on end.

On the first floor, he traversed the gray-speckled linoleum, making his way past the shiny yellow rescue vehicles loaded down with equipment. As he passed the open door to the exercise room, he heard a deep grunt followed by a loud thump, then another.

He stopped to investigate, finding Meghan standing in front of the punching bag with boxing gloves covering her hands. Oblivious to his presence, she pulled back, grunted, and threw her entire weight into another strike. The blow sent the bag swinging.

"Hey," Aiden said. "You hungry?"

Ignoring him, she landed another hit. This time the momentum nearly took her off her feet.

"Hey," he said, louder this time. "You mad at that thing?"

This time she paused and looked his way. "Sorry, what'd you want?"

Aiden rubbed at his right eyebrow. "Nothing. Just walking by and saw you in here beating up the bag."

"I'm training," she said, unlacing her gloves. She removed them and gave them a toss into the box by the lockers.

"Training for what? A fight?"

She nearly growled in his direction. "No, not a fight. I simply want to be fit and strong. Is that a problem?"

Aiden held out open palms. "No, no problem. Carry on." He walked away, puzzled. Meghan was undeniably in a bad mood. He knew better than to poke an angry bear.

In the kitchen, he found Grant Costa and Jeremy Hogan at the table. Mike Carr, the HR director, stood at the stove. When he saw Aiden, he held up his spatula. "Making grilled cheese sandwiches. Want one?"

Aiden's stomach suddenly growled. When was the last time he'd eaten? "Sure," he said. He moved to the cupboard for some plates. "You guys eating?" he asked his teammates.

Grant shoved the final bite of a Snickers candy bar into his mouth. "You bet."

Jeremy laughed. "When have you ever known Grant to pass up food?"

Aiden grabbed the plates and a bag of unopened potato chips off the counter and walked them both over to the table. "Hey, anybody know what's up with McCord?"

Jeremy shook his head. "No idea. She's as mean as a wild cat, though. I asked how her evening went last night and she nearly bit my head off."

"Must be PMS," Grant said, wadding up the empty candy wrapper.

The remark earned him a look from Mike. "Hey, watch it. Overtures like that can be misconstrued. For that reason, all references of that sort are prohibited in the workplace," he warned.

Grant rolled his eyes. "Okay, allow me to reword my evaluation of the matter. McCord is cranky with a touch of psycho." He stood and aimed for the waste can, dunking the wrapper without hitting the edges. He threw his arms above his head. "Score!"

Mike juggled a spatula stacked with hot sandwiches to the table and passed them out.

Grateful, Aiden lifted his from his plate and took a large bite. He barely chewed before swallowing, then took a second bite. "This is good, Mike. Thanks."

A low, howling moaning sound came from the direction of the window. "Looks like we need to caulk our window frame. That wind is whipping outside."

"I'll add it to the list," Aiden promised, shoving the remainder of the sandwich inside his mouth.

Suddenly, all of their cell phones buzzed. At the same time, the alarm went off out in the station. Red lights lit up and flashed off and on.

Aiden shoved his plate aside and grabbed his phone. "Looks like we've got a call."

Grant frowned. "A shark bite victim. Honolua Bay."

Everyone but Mike raced for the lockers. They grabbed helmets and their gear and raced through the station, climbing into their two rescue vehicles. Aiden drove unit number one.

Next to him in the front seat was Meghan. The two new guys rode in the back.

No matter how many times Aiden had responded to a call, he still felt his stomach clench and beads of sweat on his back. This job carried huge responsibility, and even more now that he was captain.

Even so, he was a member of a well-trained team. They had all put in hours of mock rescues and taken grueling physical tests. After a round of twenty-five pull-ups, SAR team members ran a timed one-hundred-yard obstacle course while carrying two fifty-pound dumbbells. Then they were timed while they marched one mile carrying a forty-pound rescue litter—the caged metal stretcher used in air and sea rescues. Team members then had to get in their rescue harness, swim fins, and snorkel for a one-third of a mile solo swim, followed by another third pulling along a volunteer "victim"—to be completed in less than twenty-seven minutes.

In Aiden's opinion, his team was the best around. They were ready for anything.

Still, shark bite situations posed a particularly dangerous scenario, especially when the victim remained in the water. Not only were they racing against time to get to the victim before they possibly bled out—but the possibility of another hit to one of his team members was imminently possible. This required special care and a team who remained level-headed at all times.

They would work alongside Coast Guard and county medical emergency workers, but the people dispatched directly into the water in these situations was often the SAR team.

It took less than a half hour to reach the remote area in Honolua Bay where the incident was reported to have occurred. A small crowd had gathered on the shoreline, anxiously awaiting the rescue. Thankfully, the Coast Guard already had one of their bright-yellow helicopters in the air.

Aiden slammed his vehicle into park and they scrambled

out. "McCord, you take the Wave Runner." He motioned to the other two. "You're with me."

They assembled the water rescue equipment they'd need—rescue tubes made of high-density foam, ring buoys, a rope, a backboard, and a medical bag. All were tossed into a bright orange rescue raft. Together, they pulled the raft from the trailer and heaved it to the water's edge.

Next, they quickly donned high-buoyancy SAR vests and yanked neoprene hoods over their heads, then pulled on their gloves and scrambled aboard.

"Hurry," Aiden shouted. "Let's go!"

Palms along the shoreline bent to the force of the winds whipping the ocean water and causing white caps on waves Aiden would guess to be at least four to six feet high. Not the highest swells he'd encountered, by far, but still a respectable obstacle to their efforts.

As the engine roared to life and they set out, bucking the waves, Aiden glanced skyward. Dread mounted as he noted the dark color forming to the east. Honolua Bay was on the northern tip of Maui, on the windward side of the island, and was subject to Kona winds, which could get dangerous.

The SAR team would have to work efficiently...and fast.

Aiden brought a walkie talkie to his ear and listened as the helicopter pilot reported the coordinates for the location of victim and his friend. He quickly calculated the distance in his mind. Four-hundred-forty yards. Aiden gunned the motor to high-throttle against the powerful waves bucking against their rescue sled.

In the distance, he spotted Meghan on the Wave Runner. She was waving wildly, signaling she'd located the victim. The voice on the other end of the walkie talkie confirmed they were close to their destination.

Aiden heard Meghan cut her motor and watched as she dove into the water with a rescue tube and a ring buoy in hand.

Using a one-armed side-stroke, she expertly cut through the ocean's surface until she reached the person in the water.

He maneuvered the rescue raft in place and tethered it to her Wave Runner. The team members scrambled into the water, loaded down with ropes, medical supplies, and a backboard.

The victim was a twenty-two-year-old surfer. His surfboard was mangled with toothmarks from the shark attack…likely a tiger shark, which were prevalent in the area, especially during and after a storm. The gray sky and the murky ocean water at the mouth of inlet leading into the bay created conditions that were perfect for a shark strike. The area could only be accessed by taking a trek on foot through lush tropical vegetation and a forest of tall banyan trees covered with long vines hanging from the limbs. The beach consisted primarily of tiny black stones and boasted of pockets of shallow water filled with reefs loaded with colorful fishes, which made the spot a popular destination for tourists wanting to snorkel. Eel spottings were reported regularly, as well as an occasional octopus.

Honolua Bay was also a favorite spot among surfers, especially when there was a north swell firing. Sadly, tiger sharks also frequented the area, causing three to four incidents per year, a few of them fatal.

Aiden swam to the victim, joining Meghan. "What've we got?" he asked her, aware the surrounding water was turning a burnished red color. A sign of danger to both the victim and to the rescuers, should another tiger shark be lurking.

"Looks like a severe gash to the leg and another to the heel. Lots of blood." She had secured a life ring under his armpits.

Aiden knew what that meant. The probability of shock setting in. "What's your name, buddy?" he asked, cradling the victim's head against his shoulder.

The kid was young, reported to be about Shane's age. "Rich," he forced out through chattering teeth.

"Well, Rich...we're going to take good care of you. Don't worry about anything. We've done this hundreds of times, and we're going to get you safely on shore. Then the emergency workers are going to get you all the medical care you need. So, you hang in there. Okay?"

Rich nodded. His face was pale, an indication of loss of blood.

After instructing his guys to load Rich's friend on the Wave Runner to get him out of danger, Aiden pulled off a glove and placed two fingers against their victim's external jugular vein. The pulse was weakened. He gave a silent look in Meghan's direction. She nodded and pulled a tourniquet kit from her bag.

The human body has, on average, between four to five liters of blood. The greatest risk in a shark attack is that of bleeding out. A victim can bleed out from an amputated limb in under five minutes. Thankfully, Rich's injuries were less severe. Still, it was apparent he'd suffered a rip to an arterial vein. Attending to blood loss was their first priority when it came to first aid.

With the help of the rest of the team, they rolled Rich onto his side, known as the recovery position. That way, if Rich lost consciousness, his airway would remain open and not blocked off.

The tourniquet was quickly placed, high and horizontal.

"You still with us, Rich?" Aiden asked, knowing they had less than three hours to get him needed additional medical care.

The guy nodded, his eyes still wide with fear.

Meghan grabbed his chin in her gloved hand. "We're going to get you safely to the hospital, do you hear me? Relax, and let us do the work. You are simply along for the ride." Her comment was meant to lighten the moment, and it hit its mark. Rich gave her a weak smile.

Over the next minutes, the Coast Guard helicopter overhead maneuvered into place above them. The blades made a whapping sound that echoed off the ocean's surface. Or perhaps that was Aiden's heart beating against his ribs.

A line lowered a basket. Their next job was to secure Rich on the backboard so he could be secured and lifted into the basket, then transported to Maui Memorial where a medical team was waiting.

The two new guys moved into place and worked to slide Rich in place. They quickly secured belts over his abdomen and upper legs. Another strap was strategically placed over his forehead and fastened, leaving little chance for movement once the helicopter would lift him to safety.

That was the first chance Aiden had to inspect the wound. The sight made his stomach somersault.

The gash on the front of Rich's right lower leg was approximately five inches in length. Aiden could see bone protruding from the bloody flesh. The kid's heel looked like hamburger meat. It was likely an amputation was in Rich's future.

Aiden closed his eyes against the image, one he knew he'd see in his dreams for nights to come. This job carried more than the weight of the equipment.

He glanced over at Meghan. Their gazes met. She had tears in her eyes.

Aiden gave her a supportive smile and she quickly looked away, wiping at her eyes with her wet sleeve.

That's when he saw the bruises. Dark, purple blotches at her wrist.

The sky opened and heavy pellets of rain immediately turned into a downpour. "Let's go. Let's go." He lifted an arm and made a circular motion, signaling to the helicopter pilot that the victim was secure and ready for transport.

The rain would not hinder the helicopter's function, but it would make visibility an issue. As soon as their shark bite victim was inside, the pilot gave the thumbs-up. The helicopter engine geared up and the helicopter lifted, its rotors causing circular waves on the ocean's surface. Aiden swam over to Meghan. Over the chaotic noise, he took hold of her bruised arm. "We need to talk," he shouted.

"Leave it alone, Briscoe. It's none of your business," she warned. She turned away. Using a well-practiced crawl stroke, she swam to the Wave Runner, climbed on, and sped away.

25

Christel set the box containing the new air fryer on her dining table and grabbed the roll of wedding paper her mother was good enough to give her. "Here, honey," she'd said, thrusting the wrapping paper into her hands. "I know you don't have a lot of time to go shopping."

Truth was, neither did her mother. While they'd contemplated the issue off and on for a couple of years, recently, their financials had been steady enough to move forward with upgrading the golf course at Pali Maui.

On top of their regular operational responsibilities, the decision to take on such a huge project would heap hours of work on top of both of them. Katie would help, of course. Their mother had made it clear she wanted Katie to take on more and asked Christel to include her in the preliminary finance meetings. She'd explored many funding options. In the end, it was clear Pali Maui did not have the resources to go the project alone. They'd need an investor willing to make a short-term commitment—a bridge loan—to help shoulder the financial burden until the grand opening, when revenue would finally materialize.

The idea of all the work that lay ahead made her tired just thinking about it.

After cutting a large swath of wedding paper and laying it out on the table top, Christel centered the box, and grabbed the tape, and held it in her mouth as she folded the paper around her gift. She was about to tape one end when her phone rang.

"Hey, Mom," she said, answering. "What's up?"

Her mom told her all about her day with Uncle Jack. They'd gone to the Maui Swap Meet.

"Oh? I haven't been in so long," Christel told her, abandoning her wrapping project and heading for the refrigerator. She pulled out a can of soda and popped the top with one hand, a skill she'd mastered some time ago due to the extraordinary amount of time she spent on the phone. "Did you find anything good?"

She plopped onto her sofa and kicked her feet up onto her coffee table as she listened to her mother recount all the things she'd come home with.

"Oh, and I found these wonderful little wedding favors. I know Shane and Aimee aren't planning anything extravagant, but it's the little things that make the day so special, regardless of the size of the celebration."

"What'd you find?"

Her mom started to tell her, then paused. "I know—let's FaceTime so I can show you."

The suggestion tickled Christel. Her mother was no novice when it came to technology. Unlike many women her age, she didn't shy away from using all the features on her computer and on her phone. Still, her mom wasn't often one to enjoy screen time and reminded Christel of that fact every time Christel tried to set up a video meeting.

They connected, and through the tiny screen, Christel could see the elation on her mother's face as she held up miniature soaps in the shape of plumeria blooms.

"They look so realistic, don't you think?" her mother asked. "And the smell...I don't know how the artisan captured the sweet aroma of my favorite flower."

"Sounds like great gifts for all the female guests, but what about the men?" Christel took a drink from her soda can.

"Men bathe, too."

"I know," Christel argued. "But plumeria? I'm not sure Evan would appreciate walking around the hospital smelling like flowers."

Her mom waved her off. "Don't be silly. Of course, there are a variety of scents, including some a little more manly. I added some with Bay Rum. That's more masculine, don't you think?"

"What does Aimee say about all this?" Christel gently prodded.

Her mom's hand went to her chest as her expression formed a mock look of shock. "You aren't accusing me of overstepping my bounds? I am not one of those mothers who meddles in the affairs of their children. I'm simply trying to be helpful." She paused, and a concerned look crossed her face. "Goodness! You don't think I'm overstepping, do you?"

Christel laughed. "No, Mom. I don't. Just make sure you check with Shane and Aimee before moving forward with any consequential plans. They've made it pretty clear that they want this ceremony to be very low key and simple."

Her mother shook her head. "Well, they say that...and then they go and invite that realtor woman to help them with things. She's anything but understated."

"What are you talking about?"

"Wimberly Ann Jenkins. She's the realtor Shane and Aimee worked with to find their house."

"You mean the one who has the hots for Mig?" The subject matter of Wimberly Ann's pursuit of their farm manager had been discussed at the dinner table...twice.

"Yes, that one," her mom confirmed.

Christel groaned. "I don't want to be mean, but she has very peculiar taste when it comes to her wardrobe and hair style. She reminds me of an older version of that celebrity...what was her name? You know, the one who married the rich old guy in Texas and then became an overnight television personality."

Her mom smiled. "You mean Anna Nicole Smith?"

"Yes. That's her. I think *Entertainment Tonight* aired at least eighty hours featuring her life story and rise to fame. That's not even counting the other stations or the cable tabloid shows. And all because she dressed to accentuate her generous assets. Judging from the way she dressed, she had to have come down with more than a few colds."

"Well, we may not share the same sense of fashion style, but Mig is highly impressed. Wimberly Ann showed up multiple times over the past couple of days, always with the excuse of dropping off final paperwork or tax documentation to Shane. Each time, I've noticed she lingers until Mig makes his way over, which is also manufactured, if you ask me. It's rare Mig finds need to come over to the offices during the daytime. Yet, somehow there he is every time she shows up."

Christel finished her cola and set the empty can down. "Ah, that's sweet. Mig's been alone for a lot of years. She may not be our pick, but who can control the heart? Right?"

"He's been single for exactly—well, let's see..." Her mother placed a finger against her mouth, mentally calculating the years. "His thirty-year-old daughter, Leilani, was eleven years old when her mother took off for better pastures. Sadly, when it comes to men, that woman has been rotating fields for years." She shook her head. "Anyway, Mig has been on his own for nearly twenty years. But, back to the wedding. I learned Wimberly Ann offered to help them...and they are letting her!"

Christel and her mom exchanged worried glances. They both knew what that could mean. Still, Christel wanted to be positive and encouraged her mom to look at the bright side of things. "In her line of work, Wimberly Ann must know a lot of people. Maybe she gets discounts."

"Like Shane's been on a budget."

"True," Christel replied. Her little brother had spent a great deal on the ring and on a down payment for a house. To her estimation, he'd drained his inheritance from their father. "Well, it's their wedding, their decision...right?"

"Of course, you're right," her mom immediately agreed. "As long as Shane and Aimee are happy, nothing else really matters."

MIG SAT on the edge of his bed with trembling hands as he reached for his phone. *You can do this*, he told himself. He picked up his phone off the bedside table, then quickly put it down again. Shaking his head, he grabbed it again. His other hand lifted the business card, and he stared at the number.

Before he could chicken out again, he quickly dialed her number.

And waited.

By the third ring, he'd decided to hang up when he heard a click on the other end of the line. "Hello?" Her voice came through the phone, smooth as that expensive bourbon Ava gifted him each Christmas.

He struggled to clear his throat. "Uh, hello. This is Mig... Miguel Nakamoa," he quickly clarified.

"Mig? What a surprise," she drawled. "A very pleasant surprise. I had almost given up on the notion you might ever use that telephone number I gave you."

His heart pounded so hard, he was afraid she might hear it through the phone. He swallowed. "Uh, yeah. Is this a bad time?"

"Of course not, darlin'. It's a perfect time."

Mig scrambled to remember what he'd planned to say. Unfortunately, now that he was on the line with Wimberly Ann, his mind was a complete blank.

The last time he remembered being at a total loss for words was when Esther told him she was leaving.

His wife's—er, he meant ex-wife's—decision had not come as a total surprise. Esther was never one to remain faithful. It was unspoken knowledge between them that her late-night pinochle games with girlfriends did not include playing cards or scorecards…or even girlfriends. Not knowing what to do, he'd looked the other way. Denial can be cathartic when you're too scared to do anything else.

The fighting was the worst. Esther had the ability to slice his heart with her words. She'd picked daisies to carry down the wedding aisle…later to claim during an argument that she had come to hate daisies. "They're just a weed that will take over a garden if you don't trim them back. If I'd have had better sense, I'd have picked something more elegant."

And there was the rub. He could never meet up to her impossible expectations. In her head, Esther lived a fairytale and he was certainly not her prince. Apparently, neither were the second, third, or fourth guys. Last he'd heard, she was still chasing the royal coach waving her damn glass slipper.

No one in his family had ever gotten a divorce. He came from a line of long-term unions. It was not unusual for his clan to celebrate fifty-year anniversaries. Nakamoas believed splitting from your spouse was shameful. He hung on for as long as she would stay, particularly for Leilani's sake. A young girl needed her mother.

Sadly, Esther wanted their daughter even less than she wanted him.

Many people, including Ava and Lincoln, told him they might both be better off without her. Yet, when Esther declared their marriage was done, the idea nearly kicked him in the gut.

There was no worse feeling than not being wanted.

"Mig? You still there?"

Wimberly Ann's voice pulled him back to the conversation. "Yeah, I'm here. Uh, I'm sure you're wondering why I'm calling."

"I'm not assuming anything, Mig. Only hoping," she purred.

Her remark gave him the courage to continue. "Well, being you love vintage cars and all, I was hoping you might want to go for a ride sometime. With me, in my Bel Air." He felt himself flush, his hands grow a bit clammy.

"Oh, Mig. I'd love to! When?"

When? He hadn't really thought that far ahead. "Any evening this week? Maybe Friday?" He swallowed. "I mean, if that works for your schedule."

"Friday is fine. Want to pick me up early...say, five o'clock? We might even grab a bite to eat."

Mig felt like a weight was lifting from his chest. "Yeah, that would be great!"

"Okay, see you then. And, Mig?"

"Yeah?"

"I'll be counting down the minutes."

She hung up, and Mig was left holding his phone. Slowly, a smile nipped at the corners of his mouth.

He was going on a date.

26

Aiden sat at his kitchen table, ignoring the half-finished flooring. He'd had every intention of restarting his house renovation after recuperating from his accident. Shortly after, he was awarded with a promotion at work and his life blew up in all kinds of ways, none of which left time to finish all his plans. So he'd simply left them, intending to finish later, a situation that drove his sister, Katie, crazy.

"Let me step in. I'll do it for you," she offered. "You can't just live in a mess. Let me finish all these projects—your kitchen floor, the shower tile, the decorating."

"That would be a no," he told her. "I'm on a budget and you don't know how to close the purse strings." He saw the look on her face, but it had to be said. Sure, he had the money his dad left, but he had taken Christel's advice and invested it in long-term money market funds. "A penny saved is a penny earned," she reminded, sounding like someone twice her age.

Aiden considered talking to his sisters about what he'd seen on Meghan's arm, the deep bruises...and what he suspected.

And he still might. First, he wanted to wrap his head around what he was dealing with.

He leaned and opened his Mac. With a few clicks, he brought up his search engine. Not sure exactly what he was looking for, he simply typed *suspected physical abuse*. The phrase seemed like a good beginning point.

A long list of articles immediately appeared. Aiden scanned the options and clicked on a link, opening it. He started reading.

Over the next hour, he learned a lot. As he suspected, there was a lot of shame wrapped around these situations. Few victims liked to admit they were being physically abused or mentally manipulated with fear.

The statistics were staggering.

Government agencies estimated 1.3 million women were victims of physical assault by an intimate partner each year. Not only did this result in a severe rise in depression and suicide attempts, but the problem took a huge toll on productivity in the workplace with victims of domestic violence losing nearly eight million days of paid work per year in the United States, resulting in a $1.8 billion loss in productivity for employers.

Aiden shook his head and ran his hand through his hair, considering how to apply that to Meghan. Frankly, he couldn't imagine such a strong woman like her putting up with that. Most men were a little bit afraid of crossing her, for what she might choose to do in retaliation. "Hmph," Aiden muttered out loud. "She could kick my butt in a match, any day."

So, was he crazy? Was his imagination taking off on him, simply because he jumped to conclusions too quickly? True, he didn't like that dude she was hanging with. Aiden had a good gut, and his was telling him Ron Culvane was nothing but trouble. So, when he spotted that dark-purple bruising, had he made assumptions based on his dislike for the guy?

He clicked on, reading more.

What he learned had him stunned. Authorities reported narcissistic abusers often prey on someone doing well in life, someone who has their emotions under control. These abusers see someone who isn't outwardly over-emotional or weak as a challenge. It was all about gaining control and feeling superior.

Well, that was Meghan McCord to a tee...put together and not driven by feelings. Aiden had never met anyone so self-controlled, so unabashedly unwilling to succumb to emotions. The closest he'd come to seeing her show her feelings was when she visited him in the hospital after his accident. Even then, she quickly grew embarrassed and quickly wiped her tears away.

Perhaps he wasn't imagining things. This guy may have targeted Meghan. The question remained: Why was his co-worker willing to put up with such treatment? He didn't know the answer to that question, but he hoped to find out. He needed to go straight to the source and have a direct conversation.

In the following days, Aiden attempted to create an opportunity to confront Meghan with what he'd seen and talk to her about it. He wanted to lend his support. As her boss, he also wanted to ensure Maui Emergency Management did everything possible to underpin her safety.

He dropped by her office at the first chance, hoping to invite her to join him for lunch. She politely declined, saying she had errands to run. The following day, when he learned her car was going in for a new set of tires, he offered to pick her up and drive her to work. After their work day, he'd take her home. She adamantly turned him down. "No worries, Aiden. Changing tires won't take long. Frankly, I'd just as soon wait for my car and not be stranded."

Aiden didn't think it wise to approach her at work with what he saw on her arm. Since he couldn't seem to get her alone otherwise, he made a bold decision. The only one she'd left him.

Aiden pulled up to Meghan's place and cut the engine. Her car was in the driveway, a good sign that she was home. Getting out, he mustered all his resolve and headed for her front door.

Her house was not too far from where he lived in Lahaina. The single-story house was painted green with white shutters at the windows. The yard consisted primarily of concrete driveway. While neat, there were no flowers or outward adornments.

Aiden stepped up to her front door, knocked, and waited.

When there was no answer, he rapped again. A little harder this time.

Still, no answer.

Like a nosy neighbor, he leaned the side of his face against the cheap wooden door and listened. There were voices. No, wait...that was a television.

Another indication she was home. Who left the TV on if they weren't home?

Aiden stepped away from the door and rubbed at his stubbled chin. What should he do now? He couldn't very well break in to establish confirmation that she was home and not answering the door.

Movement caught his eye. He quickly diverted his attention to the window. The drapery shifted back in place.

That's all he needed.

He turned and pounded on the door. "I know you know why I'm here, Meghan. I'm not going away, so you might as well let me in." He only hoped no neighbors were watching. They might suspect she was in danger because of him, and might call the cops.

"Open up, McCord." He scowled, knowing there was little he could do if she chose to ignore his request. Still, she'd eventually have to face him at the station and answer for why she wouldn't allow him in.

Meghan must've realized the truth of that. There was a sound at the door, a click. Slowly, the door cracked open. Seconds later, the door opened wide. "What do you want, Aiden?" Defeat shaped his friend's face.

"You know why I'm here." Aiden gave a pointed look at her sleeve-covered arm. She wore an oversized sweatshirt, despite the mild island temps. "Am I right to be worried?" he gently pressed.

She released a protracted sigh and waved him inside. "Sit." She pointed to a sofa filled with unfolded laundry at one end. "Sorry, I haven't had time..."

"No worries," Aiden assured her as he took a seat. "I'm not here to evaluate your housekeeping, I'm here to help."

Meghan motioned for the kitchen. "Want a beer?"

"Sure," he said, buying a little time. He'd given the matter a lot of thought, played out various conversations in his head. Now that he was here, he felt clueless on how to broach the topic and what to say. Something told him to just speak from the heart.

When she returned, she handed him a cold can of beer and a tall frosted mug. When he expressed appreciation for the mug, she simply said, "It's the little things, right?"

He poured the beer, waiting for the frothy head to settle. Neither of them said a word as he set the remainder of the can on the table before him.

Aiden cleared his throat. "I'm not here as your boss, Meghan. I'm here as a friend." Before she could comment, he quickly went on. "As your friend, I'm deeply troubled by what I think I saw on your arm." He paused, gazed at her surprisingly blank expression. "Am I right to be concerned?"

"I can handle this," she said before downing half her beer in a single chug. She set her mug on the table. "I appreciate the sentiment, Briscoe. But I told you—I really don't need your help."

"Can you tell me what happened?" he pressed. He boldly reached for her arm and pulled up the sleeve of the sweatshirt. The sight underneath caused him to wince.

What he'd spotted during the water rescue did not reveal the extent of her bruises. Meghan's arm was marred with massive purple blotches. Even days old, the deeply hued spots appeared freshly formed. "Did someone do this to you? Was it that guy you're seeing...the one from the gym?"

She slowly nodded. "Ron Culvane. Yes, it was him."

Aiden took no comfort in having his suspicions confirmed. With the truth came an onslaught of questions. He tried not to come on too strong. "You want to tell me about it?"

"Do I have a choice?" she asked, trying to lighten the moment.

He simply looked at her. There was no lifting the heaviness those bruises represented.

Meghan grabbed a crumpled shirt off the laundry pile and busied herself folding it.

Aiden waited patiently.

She gave up and tossed the garment back on the pile, cleared her throat, and began. "Okay, okay. The truth?"

Aiden nodded, urging her on.

"I met Ron about two months ago. I'd let my bodybuilding go for lack of time. They say taking a pause can elevate the hormones that increases muscle veracity, but that had not been my experience. I was anxious to get back to a routine. The day I walked back into the gym, I was introduced to the new trainer."

Meghan gave a weak smile as her black Labrador nestled onto the floor at her feet. She bent and rubbed his head. "This is Scotch."

Aiden petted the dog's head.

Meghan leaned back against the sofa cushion. "I admit, Ron was hot. I mean, you've met him. Broad shoulders, beveled chest hard as steel. Driven. He knew the intricacies of the weight-training business and was dedicated to helping me with strength training. All characteristics I was drawn to. So, when he started paying special attention to me every time I came in, I was flattered."

Aiden took a drink from his mug, listening carefully.

"Things went on like that for a while, talking about fitness, healthy eating, the best way to emphasize muscle groups and sculpt your body. Even though I was focused on strength, who would pass up improving their appearance? I, for one, want to look good as I age. I'm no gray hair, not by a long shot. But I'm edging out of the spring chicken category. It was getting more difficult to stay in shape and taking more effort to maintain weight." She held up the mug. "These didn't help."

"Did you two officially go out?"

"Eventually. I'd had a particular long day. We were all pulling extra hours while you were laid up. I came home bushed and there was a strange car parked at the curb in front of my house. It was Ron."

"How'd he know where you lived?"

Meghan shrugged. "Not sure really. It never dawned on me to wonder about it at the time. Likely, he looked it up in the gym's records." She rubbed at the back of her neck. "I remember that, as tired as I was, a little thrill traveled down my spine when I saw him waiting in his car." She looked down the sofa to Aiden. "Don't get me wrong. I date...I mean, I can date. Lots of available men and opportunity. I just hadn't found anyone that made my toes tingle, know what I mean? When you're tired, it takes a lot to get you excited about dressing up and going out socially. Ron did that for me. Early on, he could have put a ring in my nose and led me to the moon for a cup of coffee and I'd have said yes and followed him."

"There's nothing wrong with being attracted to someone," Aiden told her.

"Yeah, that's what I reminded myself. Even when the relationship started moving far too fast. Ron was like a train speeding down the track, afraid it would miss its destination."

She drained her mug and held it up. "Want another?"

Aiden raised his half-empty glass and shook his head, no.

Meghan left for the kitchen. Her Lab followed closely at her feet. When she reappeared, she sat back down with a fresh can of beer in her hand and continued. "Ron and I saw each other nearly every day. If not at the gym, then we met for dinner. We went surfing. We went hiking. We even cooked together." She must've seen the look on Aiden's face. "Yeah, shocker. Me in the kitchen cooking."

She popped the top on her can and poured. "Like I said, things moved very fast. I dropped boundaries I typically keep in place until I know someone a long time. Then, the first hint came."

Aiden raised his glass and took a sip of his beer, watching as the features on Meghan's face strained.

"One night I was just too tired to move. We'd done a trail rescue...a missing kid. The effort was not only physically draining, but emotionally. We were all so afraid things wouldn't turn out well. The parents, well...as you can imagine, they were a wreck until we handed off the tiny boy into their arms. When it was over, all I wanted was to go home and find my bed. I had nothing left."

Aiden nodded. He totally understood, having been there before.

"I texted Ron and backed out of our plans we had that evening. I didn't hear back right away, so I told myself I'd call him later. Unfortunately, I fell asleep on the sofa, not realizing my phone was on silent." She shook her head. "The next thing I know, there was a loud banging at my door. Jerked me out of a dead sleep and scared the bejeezus out of me. That's when I also learned I had dozens of texts...all from him. Each text was getting more demanding in tone."

"And it was him at the door?"

"Yes. I peeked out the window and saw it was Ron. I immediately knew he was angry. I should have been smart enough to not open the door."

"No one expects anger to turn to anything worse," Aiden offered. "I don't need the entire story to know there's no blame on you. None."

Meghan appreciated that. "Ron barged in, yelling. In no time, I recognized he was in a full-blown rage. I've since learned that the worst thing you can do to this type of narcissistic aggressor is to ignore them."

"Did he hurt you?" Aiden was almost afraid to ask.

"Not on that occasion. His reaction shook me up, for sure. And he broke a glass. He threw it across the room when I tried to explain why I hadn't responded to his texts and calls." She drew a deep breath. "Finally, he listened to reason and calmed down. I eventually maneuvered him out the door, promising we'd go out the following evening. For good measure, I apologized profusely for skipping out on our date."

Meghan's eyes grew hard. "No way was I really going to go out with him again. Not after what I'd just seen and experienced."

Aiden released the breath he didn't even know he was holding. Meghan had the creep's number. She hadn't purposely allowed someone to treat her badly.

He pointed to her arm again. "So how did this happen?"

He saw fear cross her features. Her fingers trembled as she placed her empty mug on the table. "Well, here's where the story gets gnarly. As I backed out of the relationship, he became progressively angry. He called me day and night. Left hundreds of texts. Even showed up to work and sat in his car in the parking lot." She shook her head. "I have to admit. These antics were beginning to make me feel uncomfortable and starting to fear what he was capable of. I went to Captain Dennis, who immediately urged me to get a restraining order. I did." She looked Aiden in the eyes. "And before you wonder why Captain Dennis didn't confide in you and warn you about all this, I asked for confidentiality. He promised to honor my wishes."

Aiden drew a deep breath. He'd wished he had known earlier, but respected Captain Dennis for keeping his promise. "So, you got the temporary restraining order. He broke the TRO?"

"Not at first. In fact, I didn't hear from Ron for weeks. I quit going to the gym, of course. I changed the locks on my door. I bought pepper spray—just in case."

"Smart," Aiden said. "And then?"

"Then, out of the blue, he showed up a couple of weeks ago. The TRO had expired and I hadn't pursued it further. I hadn't heard from him so I figured he had gotten the message and moved on."

"I was wrong." She uncharacteristically teared up. "He began texting again. I blocked him. He started leaving notes taped to my car when I was grocery shopping. I spotted him at a nearby table in a restaurant. It became clear Ron was stalking me. I made another call to law enforcement. Immediately, a court date was scheduled for a hearing on a second restraining order. That's when I came home and found my dog's cage door open. I grew frantic. Scotch was nowhere to be found. Finally, I heard a whimper. I followed the sound and found him in the shower stall with the door closed." Her expression grew angry. "No food. No water."

Aiden's eyes flew open. "He was in your house?" He quickly glanced around. Dread filled him. "What happened? Did he break in?" He held his breath, knowing he didn't want to hear the answer.

"Yes. I reported the break-in immediately and shared who I suspected. The cops showed up and dusted for prints. Apparently, Ron has an extensive rap sheet, including an incident in

Honolulu where he pushed a girl from a moving car. Nearly killed her."

That sobered Aiden. "Sounds like you're dealing with far more than a serial abuser. This individual is extremely dangerous. Your life could be in danger, Meghan."

"I'm not sure how he learned there was a warrant issued for his arrest for breaking and entering, but he showed up on the beach. I wasn't alone. There were a lot of people nearby, so I figured I was safe. Again, I was wrong."

Meghan shuddered. "I had just ridden a wave and wasn't carrying my pepper spray." She held up her arm. "I had no more than stepped from the water when I felt someone grab me. It was Ron. He said he was not going to put up with my disrespect, said he was going to teach me a lesson. He used so much force, he folded me to my knees in the sand. Suddenly, he lifted his fist. Before he could land a blow, some guy grabbed his wrist and stopped him. Thankfully, the stranger had seen what was happening and was willing to step in."

Aiden raised his eyebrows. "A dangerous thing for him to do."

She nodded her agreement. "I was thankful he took the risk. Anyway, that's the story."

Aiden stood. He ran his hand through his hair, thinking. No doubt, the situation was worse than he'd imagined. Meghan needed protection. When he stated so, she became very agitated.

"I know you want to try to be the hero in all of this, Aiden. But listen to me. This deal with Ron Culvane is my problem, and mine alone. I shared the full story with you, under duress. Now I want you to butt out. There's a warrant out for Ron's arrest. Let law enforcement take care of it. If you or the guys at the station, try to step in...one of you could get hurt. I don't want that on my conscience. You got it?"

Aiden started to argue but Meghan held up open palms,

stopping him. "I meant what I said in the water that day. Stay out of my business, Aiden."

27

Mig swiped the chamois cloth over the hood of his Chevy Bel-Air, using a polishing compound to shine the surface to an even glossier finish. Finished, he stood back and inspected his work.

He'd spent the better part of the afternoon spiffing the ol' girl up, inside and out. Despite maintaining her in tip-top condition, he cleaned the floor mats, vacuumed the interior thoroughly. He even steam-cleaned the doorjambs. A special product was applied to the leather seats and another cream to the dashboard and steering wheel. He wanted this car to be in ace condition when he picked up Wimberly Ann.

He'd taken a rare afternoon off, which raised both Ava and Christel's eyebrows in surprise. "Time off, Mig? Will wonders never cease?" Ava said, patting him on the back.

Christel piped up. "You're not going to the doctor? Are you sick?"

Laughing, he shook his head no. "Just some..." He paused. "Some personal time."

Ava and Christel quickly exchanged glances. "Oh...I see,"

they nearly said in unison. Christel poked her finger in his direction. "You're going to see that real estate lady."

Understanding dawned on Ava's face. "Oh, Mig. Is that true?"

When he wouldn't confirm, one way or another, they both held to their assumptions and launched into warnings. True, they were both happy for him, but concern followed. "Be careful," Ava cautioned. "Go slow."

Again, he laughed. "I think nearly two decades is going slow enough."

Mig understood their concern. He did. He'd experienced firsthand what could happen if you chose the wrong woman. He wasn't about to go down that route again.

Yet, there was something about Wimberly Ann Jenkins that drew his attention. Sure, she was really nice to look at. Her smile was what attracted him most. But it wasn't only her appearance that caught his eye.

Wimberly Ann seemed genuinely interested in him. Do you know how that makes a guy feel? To be sought after?

When she expressed a love for vintage cars...well, that was simply a sign. Not only was she pretty, and smart (her website said she'd sold millions of dollars of real estate!) but she appreciated what he was interested in.

Esther never gave a lick of concern for anything that mattered to him. She hooked him, married him, and then tossed him away like a rotted fish. The times he tried to talk to her about things she enjoyed were met with shallow waters.

He suspected, this time, he was casting in deeper currents.

Mig swept the cloth across the top of the front bumper, for good measure. Satisfied, he tucked the chamois into his back pocket and headed for the house.

He lived in the biggest of the work shanties. Not only was it convenient to his duties at Pali Maui, but he'd raised his daughter there, close to Ava and her bunch. The Briscoes were like family. He'd relied heavily on them while raising Leilani on his own. He wouldn't have had a clue about prom dresses. Ava and her girls stepped up. All he had to do was hand over the cash.

It's said it takes a village to raise a child. In his case, that was particularly so.

Mig showered and brushed his teeth. He glossed his black hair into place with some fancy hair cream he'd ordered off of Amazon, splashed some cologne across his neck, and then wandered to his closet. It wasn't like he had to sweat a decision. His wardrobe consisted of several pairs of jeans, and a dozen or so button-down shirts...most with short sleeves. One suit hung in the back of his closet, apparel reserved for weddings and funerals.

Mig donned his newest jeans and a tropical print shirt, not something he often wore to work. As he buttoned up the fabric, he couldn't help but let his mind drift back to Wimberly Ann.

He knew little about her, really. Yes, she appeared to be a helluva realtor, but he didn't know if she'd been married or had any children. Where did she grow up? Did she prefer steak over seafood? There were so many things to discover.

Mig glanced at his bedside clock. He'd have a chance to get better acquainted in less than two hours.

When the time came, Mig climbed in his car and headed in the direction of the address printed on the business card she'd given him. Apparently, she officed out of her home. Wimberly Ann lived in an area north of downtown Lahaina known as Napila-Honokowai.

She opened her front door, immediately exclaiming, "Perfect timing!"

When his eyes raised with surprise, she giggled. "I just fixed me a little cocktail-poo. Want one?" She looped her arm in his and pulled him inside. "I make the best old-fashioned. The secret is I put a lot of honey and fresh-squeezed lemon."

Wimberly Ann showed him to the sofa. "You just wait right here," she said, not letting him get a word in. "And I'll make you one."

Mig couldn't help but smile. Wimberly Ann was vivacious and so full of life. He didn't think she had a sad bone in that pretty body of hers. "So, I like your place." Her home was a feast for the eyes. Everywhere were shelves filled with trinkets. "I like all your stuff," he told her.

She passed him a monogramed glass filled with amber liquid over shaved ice, a twist of orange peel and a dark red cherry. As she handed off the cocktail into his hand, she pulled him from the sofa and walked him to one wall filled with display shelves. "See here? This is my grandmother's salt and pepper shaker collection. I've added to it, of course, as did my mother before me." She pointed to one particular set, two tiny glass toilets. "Check out this pair. The seats lift and you shake out the salt and pepper." She laughed. When she did, her eyes sparked like the stars.

"What about all these?" he asked, pointing to a set of tiny ceramic feet printed with "I walked my feet off in Georgia." There was a fried egg and a piece of toast, an elderly man and woman sitting on toilets reading the newspaper, a hamburger and a hotdog, and a naked man and woman with holes in their private parts where the seasonings would come out.

She saw him looking at the couple and laughed. "Never hurts to be a little naughty, don't you think?"

Mig was flustered, unsure of how to respond.

That made her laugh even more. "Come see my Dalmatian collection." True to her word, she had an entire bookshelf filled with spotted items. There were spotted hats, spotted fabric napkins, a spotted wallet, and spotted dinnerware...and much more.

Mig shook his head. "That is something. Did you collect all this yourself?"

Wimberly Ann nodded. She pointed to a spotted apron. "Started with this. It was a Christmas gift from my mother." She turned to him. "Most people just see all this stuff as clutter and junk. To me, it is a cache of memories. Of things owned by family who have passed on, of trips taken, of events and celebrations. Little mementos and life souvenirs."

He couldn't argue that. When described in that manner, he felt sorry he hadn't retained similar items. He might not display them, but it wouldn't have hurt to tuck them away in a box in the back of his closet where he could take it out and look once in a while. He told her that same thing.

"Ah, honey...no need feeling sad about it. Start now. Pick something you love and just keep adding items until you have a set of those objects. I think your idea of keeping them in a box is a good one. At least you wouldn't have to dust as often."

He wandered across the room to the fireplace hearth. It still confused him why any builder would add a fireplace to a house here on the island. Maui's record low was only sixty degrees, and that was back in the seventies.

Across her mantel were frames with photographs. The ones in the center caught his eye first. There were six matching frames. Each held a photograph of Wimberly Ann in a wedding gown. Six different dresses.

He turned to her, puzzled.

"Oh, honey. Yes, that's me. I always loved being a bride." She placed her manicured hand on his arm. "I was married to my first husband less than a year when he was killed in a possum hunt. Our neighbor was a really poor shot. It was an accident, of course. Didn't make it any easier."

Before he could voice his sympathies, she pointed to the second frame. "In my grief, I married his brother. Though they looked so much alike, the similarities stopped there." She looked over at Mig. "Let's just leave it at that. The third one was a really nice guy, but he had a gambling problem. Moved me to

Las Vegas and less than six months later, we were homeless and destitute. Thankfully, the housing market in Vegas was hot at that point. That's when I learned I was good at selling real estate."

She took a sip of her cocktail. "Unfortunately, he thought my success provided opportunity to bet on the horses. I had to end the marriage, or be forever destitute."

Wimberly Ann ran her fingers over the fourth frame. "Unfortunately, my fourth husband passed away, too...of a heart attack. And the fifth wanted to have a girlfriend on the side...or two. The sixth, now he was a gem. Sadly, he still loved his ex-wife and couldn't seem to let go. When he re-enlisted and took an assignment overseas, we agreed to part ways. Two weeks after our divorce was final, he remarried his first wife. I hear they are still together."

She turned to face Mig. "Some might say I've been unlucky at love. I cling to the notion that I've been loved. Even if things didn't turn out like I'd hoped, I never regretted trying to find *the one*." She winked. "And you have to admit, I looked really pretty in those wedding gowns."

Mig felt his heart swell.

He loved her perspective. Most people never understood why he stayed with Esther as long as he did, especially given her unfaithfulness. Like Wimberly Ann claimed, love was worth the effort, even if things became arduous and complicated...even heartbreaking.

She seemed to sense his quiet resolution and dropped her head against his shoulder.

They finished their cocktails. Wimberly Ann pulled the empty glass from his hand. "Now, what about that ride?"

Minutes later, Mig opened the car door for her. She slid inside and sighed with appreciation at the all-white interior. "Oh, Mig. This is breathtaking. The restored dashboard. These leather seats, soft as a baby's butt. Even the hardware gleams."

Mig smiled like he'd just been given the man-of-the-year award. "I take care of her," he said, proudly.

Wimberly Ann stroked the dash. "It certainly shows."

"You should see under the hood. Aluminum heads. Tunnel ram intake. And, dual Holley Carburetor."

She clapped her hands with glee. "Can't wait."

They drove for hours, enjoying the way the car's engine purred, but also enjoying learning about each other. Wimberly Ann had no children. She had wanted them, but was never gifted with a pregnancy.

Surprisingly, she didn't care for dogs. She did love hotdogs. "With lots of mustard and chopped onions," she reported.

Mig shared he loved a good game of backgammon. Often, he coerced one or more of the workers to sit with him under the shade of the pergola located by the gift shop where they'd set up the board and play, vying to *bear off*...thereby securing a win.

"How long have you worked at Pali Maui?" she asked as he maneuvered the turns on the road edging along the northwest coastline. The car windows were open to breathtaking vistas of ocean stretching for as far as you could see.

Mig rubbed at his chin. "Let's see, Esther was pregnant when I first started. I was a packer back then. So, what's that? Over thirty years."

Her brows lifted in surprise. "Thirty years? Wow."

He nodded. "Seems like yesterday. Ava's dad was alive then. Robert Hart—that was his name—he relocated to Maui from San Diego after his wife died. He had two daughters, Ava and Vanessa, and a son named Jack. All now still live here in Maui." Mig braked for a car ahead of them, loaded with tourists. Some had binoculars pointed out their open windows. "Mr. Hart passed and left Pali Maui to his children. Ava bought them all out and continued to run the flailing operation, turning it into a thriving business. It's been an honor to be by her side."

"And Ava's husband died late last year?"

Mig nodded. "Yes. Sad situation, all around." He didn't say more. There was no reason to air someone else's dirty laundry. He admired Ava too much to gossip about her husband's uncovered infidelity.

Instead, Mig explained what being plant manager entailed, how he oversaw nearly all the operations, including the planting and harvesting of the pineapples and other cash crops. "Like I said, the Briscoes are like family."

"I certainly enjoyed working with Shane and his fiancée to find a house. I think they are going to be very happy. I can't wait for the wedding."

"You're invited?" Mig asked.

She confirmed that she was, that she was even helping with some of the arrangements. "I love weddings," she said, a bit breathless.

He braved rejection and looked over at her. "Do you want to go together? I could pick you up?" The question dangled like an over-ripe papaya. "I mean, if you want. No worries if you'd prefer to—"

"Yes," she said, interrupting. "I'd love that." She leaned and snuggled against his arm. Wimberly Ann laughed. But then she leaned in even closer and pressed a small kiss on his cheek.

With a will of its own, his arm went around her shoulder, holding her tight against him. And just like that, his empty heart filled to overflowing.

28

Once each quarter, Maui Emergency Services conducted training programs designed to simulate real life situations and provide the staff and volunteers needed skills to respond. As station captain, these training sessions were Aiden's responsibility. Team member attendance was mandatory.

Today, a wrecked Toyota had been towed in and would be set on fire with trapped dummies. Employees from the local fire department would help conduct the training.

Aiden scanned his clipboard and checked off two names—Grant Costa and Jeremy Hogan, two highly skilled rescue workers who were on staff and who had helped rescue him from his earlier boating accident. Aiden knew he could count on the two of them to raise the bar for everyone who followed by putting in 100 percent effort.

Grant rolled up his sleeves and donned his fire protection gear. "Stand back and let me show you how it's done," he bragged.

Aiden glanced over at Meghan. She had a sour look on her face. No doubt, she was put out to be on second string. He'd never met anyone so competitive, so focused on proving herself in every situation. Which is why Aiden was sobered by the fear he'd seen cross her face the other day when she recited her story about Ron Culvane.

Aiden had been at a loss as to how to handle the situation. Sure, as a friend, he'd step right in the middle of that guy. As captain of the station, he knew to follow protocol. Problem was, nothing in the manuals or online directly addressed SAR's responsibilities when it came to abuse of an employee outside their work hours. There seemed to be information directed at harassment in the workplace, but that was not the situation with Meghan.

Given that, he'd swallowed his pride and put in a call to Captain Dennis, his predecessor.

"Well, if this isn't a surprise!" he said upon answering. "How are you, Aiden?"

"Great, Captain Dennis. Sorry, I mean, Dennis. Old habits die hard. How are you and Edie and the kids? Are you enjoying Montana?"

His former boss told him things had never been better for him and his family. "I should have done this years ago when I was first eligible for retirement," he said. "Drank coffee this morning watching a moose!"

"Ah...that's a far cry from Maui."

Dennis agreed. "Well, you aren't calling to chit chat. What's up?"

Aiden took a deep breath. "It's about Meghan...and that guy named Ron Culvane. He's been giving her trouble again."

"Ah, I was afraid the situation might escalate."

"It has," Aiden confirmed. "And I need some advice."

Aiden reiterated the entire situation, reminding Dennis how Meghan had been attracted to Ron Culvane after meeting him at the gym. He described how quickly things soured, then escalated. Finally, he told his former boss about the bruises on Meghan's arm.

"So, you believe she's in danger?"

Aiden took a deep breath. "Yes, I do. I don't put anything past this guy. I looked up information in our manuals and online and found nothing definitive on how to address a staff member being physically assaulted. I'm prone to believe there's a line between personal and workplace. Something nags this one has a lot of gray area. Frankly, the stalking is what worries me most."

Dennis cleared his throat. "From what I know, the guy has a pretty wicked past. I worry what he's capable of. "

Aiden agreed. "Do I need to do anything at the station in light of the potential danger?"

Dennis paused and gave the matter some thought. "Well, you're right. There is nothing in writing concerning this particular situation. However, there's a good amount relating to station security, especially in shooting scenarios, etc. Off the cuff, I'd say this matter falls under that security umbrella. Tell you what, I am friendly with a guy named Barney Marler. He's an expert on stalking and abuse. Let me put in a call, see what he recommends."

"Thanks, Dennis."

"No problem, Aiden. We'll talk soon," he promised.

Just knowing Dennis was getting the information he needed lifted a big weight off his shoulders.

Aiden pulled the clipboard from under his arm and placed the walkie talkie to his mouth. "Good job, guys." He glanced at the clipboard again. "Meghan and Jud, according to the roster, you're up."

At the end of the training simulation, Aiden waved in his team. "All right, let's huddle."

Team members and volunteers assembled around Aiden, soot streaks on their faces and smelling of smoke.

"You did a good job out there. All of you." Aiden slapped the back of his clipboard against his open palm. "Proud of the effort. Look, it's getting late." He glanced up into the late-afternoon sky. "Let's get in the station and clean up. Anyone who's up for it, join me for dinner. Maui Emergency Services is paying."

Jud slapped Meghan on the back. "You were impressive out there. Dislodging the windshield in order to get to the trapped victim was brilliant."

Aiden's and Meghan's eyes met. Both of them knew that step was clearly delineated in the training materials the fire department had handed out at the beginning of the session. Aiden made note on his clipboard to remind everyone to review the safety brochures again...and often.

Inside the station, the individuals who had returned from the simulation lined up for showers. Everyone except Meghan. She climbed the metal steps and headed for her office.

Minutes later, a scream tore through the air, echoing off the rafters.

Aiden's heart lurched into his throat. The scream came from Meghan's office.

He rushed for the stairs, taking them two at a time. Grant and Jeremy followed.

At the doorway into Meghan's office, he skidded to a stop when he saw Ron Culvane. Ron held Meghan's hair in his fist and had her head pressed against the floor with his boot resting on the side of her face. In his opposite hand, he held a Smith & Wesson M&P9 pistol.

"You think you're going to disrespect me and get away it?" he growled down at her.

Aiden froze. He waved his hand, motioning for the other two to stay back. Over the open railing, he could see Jud below. He pulled out his cellphone and dialed.

Aiden predicted it would be at least twenty minutes before

law enforcement would show up, hopefully without sirens blaring. He didn't need this Culvane guy startled into doing something stupid.

His mind raced. So many options, all filled with dangerous consequences if things turned the wrong direction. The only alternative that seemed reasonable was to try to talk to him and stall, giving the police time to arrive.

Aiden cleared his throat. "Ron, let's talk. You don't really want to hurt anyone. Not when there's no way to escape."

Suddenly, Ron diverted the gun and pointed it directly at Aiden. "Stay back, Rescue Boy. This is none of your business."

Aiden's gut wrenched at the look on Meghan's face pressed against the floor. Tears pooled and spilled across her soot-stained cheek and onto the speckled linoleum. Had he hurt her? Or was she just scared?

Aiden flung his arms up with palms open. "Whoa, let's settle down. I'm not here to cause any trouble. Just the opposite." His voice sounded shaky, even to himself.

Why hadn't he hired extra security? Why did he think he had time to put measures in place? Ron Culvane was clearly a nut job with serious issues. He was dangerous. Aiden had allowed Meghan to be placed in this situation while at work. It was all on him to make sure she wasn't further victimized, or even killed.

The thought of the potential outcome chilled his skin.

"Look, like I said—let's talk," he urged.

Culvane's face turned dark. He grimaced in wry amusement as he pointed the gun back at Meghan. "And if I don't care to sit and have a little discussion?" He seemed to take pleasure in his position of power. To prove the point, he pressed his boot down on Meghan's face until she whimpered. "What's the matter, sister? You reassessing?" He let out an evil-sounding laugh. "Guess I'm worth some respect now, huh?"

While Aiden didn't want to exacerbate the situation, he needed to intervene. And quick!

He steadied his voice. "Ron, no one here is disrespecting you, man. Not me. And certainly not Meghan."

"Yeah? Then why did she block my texts and calls? Why did she block me from her social media accounts?" He bent and moved the gun closer to Meghan's face.

Aiden noticed Ron's hand was shaking as he transferred his finger to the trigger.

Knowing what would come next, Aiden leapt forward, airborne. At the same time, he grabbed for Culvane's wrist, diverting the direction of the gun.

BANG!

The gun discharged into the wall. Aiden rolled Culvane. Before the creep could collect his senses, Aiden drew back a fist and released a punch with enough force to break his jaw. Bone immediately crunched beneath his fingers. Aiden only hoped the sound came from Culvane's face and not his own hand.

Meghan grasped the opportunity and rolled away. She darted onto her feet, snapped up the computer keyboard, and slammed it against Ron's shocked face as he tried to climb to his feet. The force sent blood splattering the nearby wall.

Her stalker's eyes widened just before he reeled back and stumbled to the floor, unconscious.

Aiden quickly grabbed the loaded gun and emptied the chamber. He also released the breath he'd been holding, not giving in to his fear.

Commotion outside Meghan's office pulled his attention. In raced several officers from the Maui Police Department, including the captain, who had helped with his niece's issue at school. Aiden swiped his forearm across his face. "Boy, am I glad to see you guys."

They immediately seized Ron Culvane as he came to. They cuffed him and checked him over medically.

Aiden moved to Meghan who stood frozen against the wall. As he neared, she folded into his arms, shaking and crying. He smoothed her hair. "Shhh...it's over now. It's all right. You're all right."

The police led Ron Culvane out and down the metal stairs. As they did, the entire team below came out of their sheltering spots and broke into applause.

Aiden held Meghan for several minutes, and she let him. "I...I was so scared," she admitted into the fabric of his shirt.

"I know. I was, too." He continued to pat her back, comforting her.

The police captain reappeared. He cleared his throat. "Seems Ron Culvane had a long rap sheet. I'm guessing he'll be extradited to the mainland to face pending charges in a serious hit and run. Apparently, in addition to many other heinous acts, six months ago he ran over his old girlfriend when she wouldn't make him fried chicken for dinner. Broke both her legs and put her in the hospital for weeks." The captain shook his head. "A real nice guy."

Meghan wiped her eyes. "Thank you, all of you." She turned to Aiden. "Most especially you, Aiden. If you hadn't interceded, I'm not sure what would have happened." Her lip quivered. "I...I appreciate it more than I can say." She surprised him by brushing a kiss along his cheek.

Their eyes met and held. "I'm just glad you're okay," he told her. He pulled her into a shoulder hug, holding her there just a little longer than he'd intended.

Later that evening, Aiden made good on his promise to take the team to dinner. Only now, he added a round of drinks. "We earned this one, today."

Down at the end of the table, Meghan nodded. "I think I need a whole bottle. Better yet, a couple of Valium tablets with a big box of chocolate."

Aiden responded with laughter, along with the others. After

the past tense hours, it was good to see his team enjoying themselves. The crisis was over. Things were back to normal.

Or at least, that's what Aiden believed until his phone buzzed and he opened a text from his mom.

"Can you come home? The wedding's been called off."

29

Aiden heard a mumbled voice as he entered the supply warehouse. Straining to make out the words, he climbed the wooden ladder to the loft, the place where he and his little brother used to hide out so they could skip out on chores, instead playing Tetris on their Game Boys.

"Shane? You in here?"

"Leave me alone, Aiden. You can't fix this."

Ignoring him, Aiden stepped onto the loft floor and brushed the dust from his board shorts. He glanced around and spotted his brother over by a stack of shipping boxes. He was huddled with his head in his hands.

"Who you talking to?" Aiden asked as he folded down beside him.

Shane looked up miserably. His face was blotched and angry. "What? It's not enough for me to get dumped again? Now you've got to come see my lowest moment for yourself?"

Again, ignoring his brother, Aiden let his arm drop around his brother's shoulders. "She ain't worth it, man. I mean, I'm sorry and all, but who leaves their fiancé and their kid behind to chase a stupid dream?"

Shane sniffed and swiped his forearm under his nose. "It's not a stupid dream," he argued. "I mean, it must've been pretty important for her to leave us like that." He picked up an open bottle of vanilla vodka and handed it to Aiden.

Aiden declined with a shake of his head. "Or, Aimee was just that selfish," he suggested.

"That too." Shane lifted the bottle and took a long drink, which caused him to choke. He coughed, trying to catch his breath.

Aiden gently extracted the bottle from his brother's hand. "That's not going to help, you know."

"Yeah? You try feeling this low without a little alcohol in your system."

Aiden screwed the lid back on the bottle and leaned back against the wooden wall frame. Both he and his brother remained silent for several long seconds, recognizing the pain in Shane's voice. Life was full of switchbacks and towering cliffs with deep crevices.

Finally, Aiden broke the interlude. "Mom said she left a note?"

Shane let out a slight grunt. He pulled a wadded paper from his shirt pocket and handed it over.

Aiden opened the note and read.

Dear Shane,

I know you will likely never understand, but I have to go. A friend notified me that one of the studios is opening up auditions for a new sitcom. He thought I'd be perfect for the lead and had a real chance. These opportunities don't come up every day. I'm so sorry. I don't want to be a waitress for the rest of my life.

Take care of Carson.

Peace out.

~Aimee

. . .

AIDEN SWALLOWED, stunned. It was one thing to call off a wedding. It was something else entirely to leave your kid behind. He stole a glance over at his brother.

A single tear made its way down Shane's cheek.

"Hey, I hoped I'd find you two here." Aiden and Shane looked over to see Mig peeking over the top rung on the ladder. "Is this a private meeting, or is anyone welcome?"

Aiden's gaze met with Mig's. He nodded. "Pull up some floor and sit."

Before positioning himself on the floor, Mig placed a hand on Aiden's shoulder. "Would you mind if I had a word with Shane...alone?"

Aiden's eyebrows lifted. "Alone? Uh...yeah, sure." He got up, turned to his brother. "See you over at Mom's." He gave him the shaka sign and turned for the ladder.

When he was gone, Mig slipped down next to Shane. "So, I heard what happened."

Shane dropped his head into his hands. "I'm sure everyone will hear before all this is over," he moaned with a muffled voice. "Cue the drama."

Mig shrugged. "Eh, let 'em talk. It'll be interesting for a few days, then everybody will get bored with the news and move on."

Shane stared back at him, his expression filled with misery. "I thought she loved me, Mig."

"Yeah, I felt the same when Esther took off. I simply didn't understand how someone could just leave like that." He rubbed his hand through his black hair. "Back then, I thought it would have been easier if my wife had died. At least then, I could have been gallant at her funeral, worn dark glasses, shed tears, and taken Leilani aside to reveal her mother had been taken by some dreadful accident or disease. As it was, I had to wreck my daughter's heart by revealing her mother chose to leave her behind."

Mig brushed away a clump of dirt off the floor and continued, "When someone you love dies, everyone brings casseroles and sympathy. When the woman you love just up and leaves you for someone or something else, you are left with pity and avoidance. No one knows what to do or say. How could they? I mean, what do you say to someone who has just endured a hot firecracker to the gut?"

Shane banged the back of his head lightly against the wall. "Exactly. It's humiliating. Leaves you feeling sick inside. Like, seriously...gonna puke sick." Tears formed. "I bought her the best ring I could afford, got us a really nice house to live in. We were going to raise little Carson together. Now what am I going to do?"

Mig placed his hand over Shane's knee. "You're going to pick yourself up, dust off the hurt, and you're going to be the best dad you can be to that little boy. Oh, I'm not saying it'll be easy. There were some days I locked myself in the closet and just sat there, wondering how I was ever going to survive. Thank goodness I had your family's support. Without your mom, I might've had to buy feminine products. At least you won't face that."

The remark brought a slight smile to Shane's face. "No, only jock straps and condoms."

Mig shook his head. "Well, now, that's another thing. It'll be up to you to teach that boy of yours how to respect women. Raising a child is a big responsibility and you'll be shouldering the load alone. Of course, your family will be here to support you. And me. But parenting is weighty...and it's yours. As a single dad, you'll be lifting that load daily." A slow smile nipped at the corners of Mig's mouth. "Thing is, there is no greater joy. Aimee may have left and taken off for greener pastures, but you got the better end of the deal," Mig assured. "By far. The good Lord blessed you with Carson."

Shane seemed to ponder that. Finally, he nodded. "Yeah,

you're right. It would have been far worse if Aimee had taken my son with her and I lost them both. Not sure my heart could have taken it." He looked toward the ceiling and lowered his voice to barely above a whisper. "I guess I knew she wasn't all that happy, but I thought my love would be enough."

Mig knew exactly how the kid was feeling. He'd been there. "I guess sometimes, no matter how much you love someone, they just can't love you back in the same way." Mig tried to charm Shane with a wink. "You will survive this loss. You'll see."

"That doesn't make me feel a whole lot better, you know."

Mig released a tiny chuckle and patted his young buddy on the knee. "Sorry, Shane. It's all I've got."

30

Ava juggled a large sheet cake in her hands and slammed the car door closed with her hip. The cake was to have been the groom's cake, her contribution to her son's wedding. Now that the ceremony was called off, the least they could do was enjoy this raspberry chocolate cake with ganache frosting.

"Ava, there you are!" Vanessa scooped the cake up and led her inside the Banana Patch.

Immediately, the parrot mimicked her words. "There you are. There you are."

Ava grew worried. "You sure Shane is going to think this is a great idea? I mean, this was the wedding venue, and now..." She let her words drift off, thinking about the moment her kitchen door flew open and Shane stood there with a piece of paper in hand. From the wrecked look on her son's face, she'd known something was terribly wrong. Yet, she never could have guessed Aimee had fled. What kind of person would cancel two days before her wedding?

Shane was shattered, of course. Everyone had rallied around in support. Many hoping Shane was the sort to brush this off. But she knew her baby boy. He was struggling to come to grips with being left at the altar—the shame of it, of course. But also, her son had fallen hard for Aimee. That girl had broken his heart.

"Get that look off your face, Ava. Shane will be fine. Lots of marriages crumble. The way I see it, he got lucky. Clearly, she wasn't the type to commit. Therefore, no divorce in his future. No sharing half of the house and his money." She let out a dainty grunt. "It was tacky for her to keep the ring."

Ava held her tongue. She didn't need sister drama, not today. While she and her sister had gotten along fairly well in the weeks since Vanessa had shown up at her door, destitute and looking for help, there were times she'd like to place boxing tape over her sister's mouth. Ava could only hope Vanessa would get all this out of her system before Shane showed up. Her son didn't need to field quips about relationships that went sour.

"Yoo hoo! Ava. There you are." Wimberly Ann Jenkins swept through the front area and headed in her direction.

"There you are. There you are," repeated the parrot.

Ava turned and gave the colorful bird a look that could pluck feathers off the best of them. Her nerves were nearly shot. She certainly didn't need a bird picking at her last one.

Wimberly placed a manicured hand on Ava's forearm. "Don't you worry about a thing, darlin'. Me and Mig have everything taken care of."

That's when Ava noticed her farm manager standing right behind Wimberly Ann. He held his hat in his hands and had an impish look on his face. Clearly, he was infatuated with this woman.

Ava could barely understand why. Those two were as different as night and day. Shane had suggested it was her generous cleavage that attracted Mig. Ava doubted that was the only thing Mig cared about in a woman. He'd been through the wringer once. This time, he was likely looking past appearance and seeking a woman of character. While she might think Wimberly Ann was no deeper than a dime, Mig must believe otherwise. She'd respect that.

Alani and Elta arrived next, followed by Jack. Willa and Kina were out at the pond helping Halia set up for the party. Everyone important in Shane's life had gathered, wanting to lend emotional support. His simple wedding had been converted into a simple party.

Just outside the doors that led to the gardens, a woman sat poised in front of a cello. Her fingers ran the bow against the strings effortlessly. In turn, a soft and beautiful melody filled the air.

White hibiscus blooms floated in the pond water and the smell of hors d'oeuvres drew party attendees to tables laden with marinated shrimp, fruit kabobs, watermelon feta cubes, fried asparagus, and bacon-wrapped dates. Wimberly Ann's contribution had been a massive platter of deviled eggs topped with sprinkled paprika. "Just like my mama used to make," she said.

While Christel was reluctant to give them a try, Katie consumed two and exclaimed, "These are delicious." The compliment brought a huge smile to Wimberly Ann's face.

They had all been gathered for nearly an hour when Ava looked at her watch. She leaned over to Aiden. "Do you think Shane changed his mind? I should have listened to my gut. It's too soon after Aimee left."

Aiden put his arm around his mother's shoulders and told her not to worry. "He'll be here, Mom."

He proved to be right. Minutes later, Shane stepped through a beaded doorway holding Carson in his arms. He wore a pressed pair of khakis and a crisp white button-down shirt. He'd dressed his baby boy in a tiny suit, complete with a bow tie. "We're here," he announced. "Let's get this party started."

Ava watched as Shane mingled. He laughed at something Elta said. After listening to another of Jack's jokes, Shane patted his uncle on the back with one hand. Her son chatted with Willa and her friend, Kina. He hung with his siblings and smiled, seeming to have a good time. Whether he was putting on a show, she couldn't tell.

What she did know was that she was extraordinarily proud of her children...all of them. Christel, Aiden, Katie and Shane had weathered many fierce storms in the past months. Each time, they pushed past the darkness and found their way into the light.

Christel was bravely learning to love again. Physical impairment could not keep Aiden down, especially when a coworker was in harm's way. Katie lost her home to a fire, yet never lost hope. Now, Shane was moving forward despite heartache, determined to become a good dad to little Carson.

When Lincoln died, a part of Ava died with him. The discovery of his affair dropped her to her knees. Yet, though it all, she held onto joy.

None of them had expected to face such challenges, yet with arms linked together, Ava and her children met each event with grace and dignity. Hard things may have changed them, but despite everything, they remained a family.

They were brave. They were strong.

They were the Briscoes.

AFTERWORD

Well, hey everybody—Aloha!

Shane Briscoe here. Kellie and I are so glad you joined us for the third book in the Maui Island Series. This one really knocked my gut. As you now know, my wedding was called off at the last minute and I now face the task of being a single father. Goodbye late nights spent in the bars. Hello diapers!

Kellie and I can't wait for you to continue this series. There are some real twists and turns ahead. Love is in the air for the Briscoe family. Unfortunately, one of us will get our heart broken.

Friends, Kellie is writing as fast as she can. *The Last Aloha*, the fourth book, is now available for purchase. You'd better jump over to your favorite retailer and grab yourself a copy.

As an added incentive, Kellie has slipped a preview in here. Keep scrolling to read a preview of *The Last Aloha*.

Yes, I want my copy.

Make sure you also visit Kellie's website and sign up for her newsletter so you get notices when future books release.

www.kelliecoatesgilbert.com

Well, little Carson is waking up from his nap and I have to go change his diaper. Hope it's just wet, and not the other. But we'll see each other soon! When you visit the island, drop by and mom will give you a slice of her famous pineapple upside down cake. It's my favorite!

Mahalo!

~ Shane Briscoe

ACKNOWLEDGMENTS

A special word of thanks to the folks at Maui Pineapple Plantation (waving to Debbie, Lacey, Mary and Ken!) These fine folks let me hang with them and see how pineapples are planted, grown and harvested.

Did you know pineapple crowns are planted in the earth by hand? The pineapples then take fourteen to fifteen months to grow. Maui is known for wild pigs and if they break through the fencing, they can eat a football field worth of produce in no time.

The Maui Pineapples are picked to order and are the sweetest treat you'll ever pop in your mouth...no, really! I had such a fun time on the tour and learned so much. You guys were so supportive of this series and my heart is filled with gratitude.

Thanks also to Elizabeth Mackey for the fabulous cover designs, to Jones House Creative for my web design, and to my editors, proofreaders and to my best-selling author friend and critique partner, Heather Burch, who made this book so much better.

To all the readers who hang with me at She's Reading, you are a blast! I can't believe how much fun it is to do those live author chats and introduce you to my author buddies.

Finally, thanks to my readers. All this is for you!

~Kellie

SNEAK PREVIEW - THE LAST ALOHA

Chapter 1

A loud wail woke Shane Briscoe out of a dead sleep. Exhausted, he bolted up, wiped his eyes, then clamored from the tangled sheets and raced in the direction of the cries.

Carson's room was located down the hall from his own. In his hurry, Shane stubbed his toe on the door jamb and let out a loud—and very colorful—string of curse words before he remembered little ears were nearby. The upside? The powerful sound of his voice stopped the baby's cries.

Shane flicked on the light and shielded his eyes from the brightness with his forearm placed across his face. He stumbled to the crib against the wall and stepped on a rattle that had been left on the floor from their playtime together the night before. "Fu...dge!" he yelled, pausing mid-word to alter what he'd intended to say.

Carson whimpered and Shane lifted him, bringing his warm little body against his own. Immediately, wetness seeped onto his arm.

Shane groaned and headed for the changing table where

he expertly unsnapped the lower part of the onesie with one hand, took hold of Carson's little ankles with the other and lifted him up. With a deft and swift maneuver, Shane released the tiny bottom from the soaked diaper and tossed the sopped thing in the nearby can, letting the lid drop with a thud. His hand reached for the shelf on the wall and pulled down a clean diaper from the stack. In the process, he toppled the entire bunch. Disposable diapers cascaded down on his baby's head.

Shane waited for his son's renewed wails. Hearing none, he looked down. Carson's face broke into an adorable grin, as if his little boy thought his dad's clumsy antics were funny.

Shane finished diapering Carson, then lifted him from the table. He nuzzled his nose against his baby's neck, taking in the powdery, sweet smell. "You hungry, little man?"

He wandered with his son into the kitchen, the beautiful kitchen with white cabinetry and a spacious island topped with granite—the kitchen meant for Aimee. The moment she'd seen the double-door refrigerator, the gas stove with the fancy vent top...well, she'd gone nuts. She wouldn't even look at another house.

"This is the one," she'd exclaimed, clasping her hands in front of her chest like all her prayers had come true. Little had either of them known that Aimee would not cook a single meal in this new kitchen.

Instead, she'd left a note. A stupid note. An impersonal scrap of paper that had broken his heart and dashed his dreams of being a family. She didn't even have the decency to tell him face-to-face that she was walking out on their engagement...and their son.

Shane didn't know what he'd wrestled with more...anger, or the deep hurt. Both, he supposed. It hadn't gotten a whole lot better in the months since she'd hightailed it back to Los Angeles to follow her wacky dream of becoming a star. "I want to be somebody," she often claimed. Apparently, being a wife and a mother meant nothing to her.

Shane shook his head as he warmed Carson's bottle. Fame must mean a lot if someone is willing to swap their soul to get it.

He wandered into the living room, carrying his baby son and the bottle. The room had a single sofa. That was it...oh, except for the television mounted to the wall. Despite his skinny finances, if he was going to spend nights rocking a baby, he was at least going to enjoy some screen time.

He plopped onto the plush cushions, pulled a sofa blanket over the two of them, and poised the bottle in front of his baby's mouth. "You ready, buddy? Chow time."

Carson lobbed onto the bottle and ate hungrily until the formula was nearly gone. Among lots of other things, Shane still had to remind himself to pull the nipple from that tiny mouth every so often and burp Carson to keep his little tummy from cramping up.

Seconds later, Carson rewarded the effort with a loud, infant-sized belch. "Atta boy," Shane said, pulling the baby back down to his lap. He repositioned the bottle into his son's mouth.

Shane leaned his head against the cushion and closed his eyes. He was nearly asleep when he felt something on his arm.

He slowly opened his eyes. Carson smiled back at him and stroked Shane with his tiny, dimpled hand.

***

Ava Briscoe pulled the belt on her robe a little tighter and wandered to her kitchen window. She peered out at the worker shanties in the distance. Christel claimed she was overprotective of her youngest, but she liked knowing Shane was only a few hundred yards from her own front door, especially when he was hurting. Now, he and her new grandson lived in Napila-Honokowai, north of the Kaanapali beach area.

The entire family was still reeling from Aimee's decision to bail from her wedding to Shane. Worse? She'd deserted her son. How could a woman do that?

Ava shook her head in disgust. She would never understand how people could callously hurt the ones they said they loved.

As she moved to the cupboard for a teacup, something out the window caught her attention. She returned to the sink and leaned forward, trying to make out what she'd seen. In seconds, a figure stepped into the light cast from the yard pole.

Wimberly Ann Jenkins!

Ava's breath caught at the sight. She watched as Mig took hold of Wimberly Ann's elbow and guided her to her car. He opened the door.

Before Wimberly Ann climbed in, Mig pulled her close. He kissed her. The kiss was long, lasting far longer than Ava felt comfortable watching. Still, she couldn't seem to look away.

It seemed her faithful operations manager had fallen for the new realtor, a gal who resembled Dolly Parton—a woman who had been married six times!

Miguel Nakamoto was nearly a fixture here at Pali Maui, having worked at the pineapple plantation longer than anyone —nearly as long as Ava. His responsibilities included managing the fields and the packing operation, and supervising the employees. He was good at his job and highly respected. Ava was grateful to work alongside him, especially now that her husband had passed away.

Certainly, Mig had been alone for a long time. In a story that nearly duplicated Shane's, Mig's wife, who the entire family had nicknamed *the plate thrower*, left with another man when their daughter, Leilani, was only eleven.

After all these years, Ava had assumed Mig had determined he would remain a single man—a decision that was entirely understandable, given what he'd experienced.

Then Wimberly Ann arrived on the scene. In no time, Mig started acting like a smitten teenager. Ava noticed he wore cologne, even out in the fields. He urged Katie to take him shopping for some new clothes, and not just any clothes. According to their shared housekeeper, he'd tossed his work shirts and pants in the back of his closet. Mig was now wearing Rhoback polos and Tommy Bahama half-zip pullovers—in a shade of coral, no less!

At Wimberly Ann's suggestion, he made an appointment with a stylist in Wailea and had his straight-cut jet-black hair fashioned into a side part with a quiff. Wimberly Ann claimed the cut played up his thick hair.

Ava shook her head. She wanted to tell him to be careful.

Love might be heaven, but could turn to pure hell.

YES! I want this book!

Available at all retailers

www.kelliecoatesgilbert.com

ALSO BY KELLIE COATES GILBERT

THE MAUI ISLAND SERIES
Under The Maui Sky

Silver Island Moon

Tides of Paradise

The Last Aloha

THE PACIFIC BAY SERIES
Chances Are

Remember Us

Chasing Wind

Between Rains

THE SUN VALLEY SERIES
Sisters

Heartbeats

Changes

Promises

LOVE ON VACATION SERIES
Otherwise Engaged

All Fore Love

TEXAS GOLD SERIES
A Woman of Fortune

Where Rivers Part

A Reason to Stay

What Matters Most

STAND ALONE NOVELS

Mother of Pearl

* * *

Available at all retailers

www.kelliecoatesgilbert.com

Made in the USA
Las Vegas, NV
28 February 2023